Judgement Trail

At the outbreak of Civil War, regiments stationed along the Oregon Trail are posted back East to fight for the Union. Hastily assembled militia units seize control of the trail forts and wagon-trains are left vulnerable to exploitation and attack.

Halted with a broken axle, westbound pioneers Eve Maddison and Wesley Jackson encounter a mysterious frontiersman known simply as 'Stranger'. They also run up against the vicious Viperine brothers, in charge of a local militia and plotting to extort money from the stranded pioneers.

Stranger insists that everyone is judged by their actions on the trail. His philosophy of courage and self-reliance inspires Eve and Wesley to make a stand against the Viperines – and face up to some difficult truths. . . .

Judgement Trail

Rob Hill

A Black Horse Western

ROBERT HALE · LONDON

© Rob Hill 2012
First published in Great Britain 2012

ISBN 978-0-7090-9909-3

Robert Hale Limited
Clerkenwell House
Clerkenwell Green
London EC1R 0HT

www.halebooks.com

Typeset by
Derek Doyle & Associates, Shaw Heath
Printed and bound in Great Britain by
CPI Antony Rowe, Chippenham and Eastbourne

For Val and Joss

1

Eve Maddison had just finished emptying the wagon. She was young, strong and handled the heavy items with confidence despite the awkwardness of working in a long calico dress. Added to this, the wagon leaned precariously. The splintered end of the rear axle stuck out from underneath and the wheel which had been torn away lay beside it. The tailboard was down to allow unloading and only a mahogany chest, which was too heavy for one person to shift, remained inside.

Marooned on the empty prairie, Eve waited for Wesley to get back with a new axle. She killed time by stamping down a long rectangle of sagebrush and setting out the contents of the wagon as if they were inside a cabin. The Dutch oven stood where the hearth would be; sacks of rice and flour were stacked under imaginary shelves; iron bed ends and a rolled horsehair mattress marked where the bed would stand beside the drawers from the chest, which was still inside the wagon. Chairs faced each other across Wesley's trunk, which served as a table. Already, Eve was proud of their new home: they just had to get to California to build a house round it.

Standing in the centre of the imaginary room, Eve held the last of the possessions from the wagon. It was a triptych framed under glass: a photograph, a cutting from a newspaper and a handwritten letter. Which wall should she hang it on? She studied it as she had a thousand times. She loved looking at it. That was her in the centre of the photograph looking to one side as if she were examining the studio aspidistra. Wesley, close-shaven and round-faced, stood stiffly behind her and rested his hand on her shoulder. Conscious of their best clothes and unused to being photographed they both looked solemn and unlike themselves. Nevertheless they made a handsome couple. Eve smiled, remembering how the photographer had kept ducking out from under the black hood behind the camera to adjust the position of the plant which stood beside them.

It had been her idea to frame the photograph alongside the cutting and the letter. The triptych told her and Wesley's story and she treasured it. She longed to see it hanging on her cabin wall. The photograph had been taken on the day they agreed to go out West. The newspaper cutting was the advertisement from the *New York News* which had brought them together:

Man (27) of deliberate intentions, seeks female companion to accompany him on the Oregon Trail to start a life in California. He is upright, possessed of some means including a wagon and two horses. The woman must be sober, diligent, used to work and able to endure hardship. She must be clean, healthy and decent. Reply in your own hand to Box 714 at this newspaper within one week.

And the letter:

Dear Sir,

In reply to your advertisement, I am anxious to meet you with a view to joining you in the great undertaking you have planned. I am widowed, 21 years old, strong, in good health and possessed of all my own teeth.

I was raised on a farm in New York State and am used to dealing with horses and livestock, but especially horses. I believe I have the toughness required to endure the journey and to make a life out West. Cooking and sewing is my pleasure and I am told I have a companionable spirit.

I bring with me an allowance of $190.

If you care to meet me, I shall be at the Grapevine Coffee House on Canal Street between four and five in the afternoon on Friday 25th May 1859.

yours sincerely,
Eve Maddison

Dry heat had been building like a headache over the open prairie all day. For hours the low clouds hung still, the parched sagebrush stood motionless and the air hummed. Sometime during late afternoon a sense of rain arrived. Maybe the temperature dropped by a degree or the pressure of the air shifted, it was hard to tell. But there was something. A suggestion of dampness lifted by the breeze announced that the weather was going to change: there was to be an interruption to the months when the sun had tempered the ground like steel and the air tasted of dust. This was a land of absolutes, of burning days and freezing nights, of winters in which snow entombed the earth and summers when crucible heat bent the air. Everything fought for survival here, dark against light, heat against cold. The seasons were tenacious and never gave way without a struggle. There was always violence. This hint of rain meant a storm was on its way.

The canvas bonnet of the wagon moved in the breeze; Eve looked up. She sensed a change in the weather and cast her eye over the imaginary room in the cabin they might one day build. She chided herself inwardly for her foolishness as the first drops of rain fell. An Appaloosa pony secured with a scotch hobble grazing a few yards off raised his head as he felt the rain. Everything would get soaked; the rice and flour would be ruined. She had unloaded the wagon so they could lift it easily between them when Wesley returned with a new axle – now she would have to load it again.

A movement on the horizon caught her eye. A rider. Was Wesley coming back already? Her heart leapt: she hadn't expected him until tomorrow at the earliest. He would be here in an hour, maybe less. The wagon would have to be empty for them to fix the new axle; maybe the rain would pass over. A raindrop as big as a nickel splashed on her face, as if the weather was deciding whether it should break now or wait. Either way, she had to get the rice and flour under cover. She set about shouldering the sacks back into the wagon.

When Eve looked up again, the early evening light had yellowed and black clouds bruised the sky. Intermittent raindrops forewarned a storm. She scanned the horizon for Wesley and at first could not make him out against the shadowy sage. Then she realized it was not him. Now that he was closer she saw that it was not Wesley's horse. How could she have been mistaken?

Lightning forked in the far distance. Eve started to count and stopped when the dull boom of thunder came. Sheets of rain fell. She hurried to heave the mattress back under the wagon bonnet. Remembering that the water barrel was only two-thirds full she spread out all the cooking pots and took the lid off the Dutch oven. With their belongings flung in anyhow, her cotton dress soaked and clinging to her shoulders, she squeezed under the canvas to watch the rider approach.

The storm blew from the north. Daylight failed as clouds rolled overhead and a downpour scourged the parched land. It battered the wagon canvas and drenched the sage. The Appaloosa moved in close beside the wagon and stood with his head bowed. Lightning flickered along the horizon. Eve counted again; the storm was closing. Everything near the open ends of the wagon was soaked and the dampness of her dress made her shiver. A wall of rain obscured everything. The rider disappeared.

Where the linseed protection was too thin, water dripped through the canvas and soaked the horsehair mattress. Eve clambered down to fetch one of the cooking pans. Just walking the few yards outside the cover of the wagon meant she was soaked to the skin. The storm clouds lowered as if the weight of water forced them to rest on the ground; grey fog swirled around her as the downpour stung her neck and shoulders. The cooking pan in her hand rang like a cymbal. She clambered back into the frail shelter of the wagon and put the pan under one of the leaks. The deluge beat the waterproofing out of the canvass and a hammock of water which clung to the inside of the roof, showered over the food and clothes each time she moved.

Everything inside the wagon was soaked now. Eve found a blanket which was less wet than the others and flung it round her shoulders. She pulled the cotton cap off her head and started to wring out her long dark hair. Lightning flashed overhead and a fork stabbed the ground somewhere close. She had barely started to count when thunder exploded. The Appaloosa screamed and barged the wagon, rocking it until she thought it might tip over altogether. She called out to him to be calm, that it was nothing, that the storm would pass. Again, lightning ruptured the sky. The horse banged against the wagon. She worried now that the hobble would cause him to break a leg if he reared. Eve pulled the blanket round her and climbed over the tailboard to go to him.

As she rounded the side of the wagon into the whipping rain, she caught her breath. A tall, square-shouldered man stood there with one arm over the neck of the Appaloosa while he patted him gently with the other and spoke reassurance into his ear. The hobble lay at the horse's feet. The man wore a long oilskin with the collar up; rivulets of water ran off the brim of his hat. His own horse, a handsome bay, stood patiently nearby watching them. Lightning flashed again but Eve failed to count this time. The man looked her directly in the eyes. Eve turned away, pulled her cotton bonnet on to her head and jerked it tight. As thunder crashed, the man leaned into the Appaloosa's neck and drew the horse to him. The animal's breathing steadied and he stood still.

'I was comin' to do that,' Eve said.

As the thunder passed, the man released his hold on the pony and stepped aside. His oilskin fell open and showed the pair of Starr pistols in his gun belt. He looked at Eve as if he recognized her from somewhere, although they had never met. Far from being oppressive as the stares of men often were, the sense of familiarity made her feel at ease. Eve looped the Appaloosa's lead rope to the side of the wagon and picked up the hobble. Lightning flickered, but further away this time. Thunder rolled an answer.

'Who are you, mister?' Eve said.

The man patted the neck of the Appaloosa.

'Stranger,' the man said and pulled at the brim of his hat with old-fashioned politeness. Then he smiled as if he knew what she was going to say next. 'Christened

Thomas Elija Stranger. Everybody calls me Stranger.'

'Eve Maddison,' Eve said.

Stranger nodded to the Appaloosa.

'Won't be frightened now. Storm's due to blow itself out.'

The clouds lifted as light returned to the sky and the rain softened. Lightning danced for a moment but it was far off.

'Out here by yourself?' Stranger said.

To Eve this sounded more of an observation than a question; there was no compulsion for her to answer.

'My companion has rode over to Fort Dove to get us a new axle.'

'Companion?'

Usually Eve told people she and Wesley were married. In fact, that is what she had told everyone they had met since they started out, but without hesitation she had been drawn to tell this man the truth. She feared no judgement from him and for some reason she did not want him to suspect a lie.

'I don't care to go into the forts,' Eve said. She pulled her bonnet down over her cheek to make sure it covered the scar. 'Sky high prices and we don't need protection from the troopers right now.'

'Ain't no troopers there,' Stranger said. 'Been transferred.'

'Why?'

Stranger looked at her. He noticed the scar on her cheek which she had been trying to hide.

'How long you been out here? They've transferred the troopers from all the posts along the trail back East to fight for the Union, the ones that didn't desert. They weren't sad to leave, neither. Stuck out here for $11 a month and too poor to bring out their families. Germans and Irish most of 'em.'

'So who's guarding the trail?'

'Each post has got up some kind of militia till the troopers get back. The forts were flinty places before the troopers left, but now. . . .'

Stranger's voice fell away.

'Wesley's been gone more than a day,' Eve said.

'Got money to pay for his axle?'

Eve nodded.

'Got a gun?'

She nodded again.

'Then you won't have to worry.'

The rain had stopped and a shift in the clouds allowed sunlight through. Water droplets sparkled on the leaves of the sagebrush and steam rose from the backs of the horses. The Appaloosa nickered, blew through his nose and nudged up to Stranger. Stranger took off his hat and brushed the water off it. Eve couldn't tell if he was young or old. Tiny crow's feet clawed at the edges of his grey eyes and his hair was the colour of steel. His face was lined and weathered but the line of his jaw was determined and young.

Eve suddenly became aware of her tangle of lank hair hanging down from her cotton cap. She turned away and began to rub it with the blanket.

'I'll make a fire if I can find enough dry kindling,' Stranger said.

He removed his oilskin, shook off the water and

folded it. He wore a buckskin jacket, the kind frontiersmen wore in the old days before the territories were opened up. His leather gun-belt was dark with wear and sat comfortably on his hips but the Starr double actions were new. He gave the Appaloosa a last pat and turned to scour the ground for brushwood. Within half an hour, they sat in front of a spitting fire, listened to the lid of the percolator rattle and smelled coffee on the rain-freshened air.

Later, as sunlight warmed the air, Eve rigged up a line and pegged out the blankets. Stranger inspected the broken axle.

Absorbed in her work, Eve failed to notice the three riders approach from the direction of the fort until they were right on her. The fact that the men did not holler a greeting to announce themselves surprised her and when she looked round for Stranger he was not there.

The riders wore ragged beards and their clothes were dirty and unkempt; two of them wore plainsman's hats and one a Stetson. The eldest was in charge. He had a rabbit's foot on a leather thong round his neck as well as a Sioux amulet. All three reined in their horses and stared down at Eve.

'Fort Dove Militia,' the older one said. His heavy accent was not one Eve had heard before. 'Name's Landry Viperine. I'm captain, formally appointed until the regiment gets back. These here are my brothers Remy and Charles.' He paused and a smirk slid over his mouth. 'No need to tell me who you are because I already know.'

Eve felt the men's eyes on her and wished she still

had the blanket round her shoulders.

'What can I do for you?'

'Met your husband. Said he had enough money to buy wood for an axle and to hire the carpenter's shop for a day.'

Landry paused to run his tongue over his lips.

'Didn't have enough to pay the Militia Charge. Told us you were out here, though, so we thought we'd pay you a visit.'

'Never heard of a Militia Charge,' Eve said.

'Everyone pays the Militia Charge,' Landry said. He spoke lightly as if he was explaining something to a child. 'Else, who's going to keep the trail protected? Who's going to keep the fort repaired?'

Eve stared brazenly at the men. Her face was a mask while her heart raced. 'There ain't no such thing.'

'Not everyone can pay cash dollars,' Landry continued. 'We know that. We're reasonable. We take payment in kind, don't we boys?'

The others grinned agreement.

'Any kind,' Remy said.

'All kinds,' Charles said.

Choking on their laughter, the Viperines watched Eve and waited for a sign of weakness: a question about Wesley maybe, a protestation that she had no money, anything that signalled fear. She glared back and gave them nothing.

Stranger jumped down from the tailboard of the wagon and stood beside her. The Viperines' smirks fell from their faces. They straightened in their saddles and tightened their grip on the reins. They took in

Stranger's height, build, the easy way he stood and the twin Starrs which rested on his hips.

'Everybody pays before they leave,' Landry said. 'Cash or kind. That's how it is around here. Took the trouble to ride out to tell you, just like we told your husband.'

But before he finished speaking, the other two had turned their horses back in the direction they had come.

2

Fort Dove had been founded fifteen years earlier. Originally, it was a collection of sod-built houses where mountain men exchanged pelts for supplies and buffalo hunters sold hides. In the early days, the Sioux were welcomed and they traded animal skins and carvings for food during the hard winters. Anyone who had the means and the willpower to haul a wagonload of supplies out here could make a living: traders could charge high prices and hides were in constant demand at the tanneries back East.

But now things were different. Traders lost the trust of the Sioux with the measles outbreak. So many children and babies died that, grief-stricken and desperate for an explanation, the Sioux refused to believe that this tragedy could have happened by accident. They became convinced that the white men had done it on purpose. Added to this, the second generation of traders contained rogues with no understanding of frontier life who were lured out to the trading posts by the prospect of making a quick buck. They sold rotgut and rifles to the Indians, overcharged them and reneged on their deals.

The Sioux were not the traders' only victims: in addition to the usual overcharging, they cheated the wagon train pioneers by convincing them that there was no market for beef and milk cows in California and persuaded them to part with their cattle at rock-bottom prices. They then fattened the animals, drove them West themselves and sold them for a tenfold profit.

The US government heard about what was going on. When the threat of Sioux attacks on the wagon trains grew, they sent regiments to fortify the larger trading posts and guard the smaller ones. For a while the posts became peaceful, law abiding places. Now, with the troopers either gone back to fight in the war or deserted, the forts were in the hands of self-appointed militia groups who found themselves with carte blanche to extort money from the wagon trains and antagonize the Sioux.

As Wesley rode through the gates of the Fort Dove stockade, he cast his eye over the place. Round a main square were a few sod-built houses dating back to the days of the early traders; a saloon tent; a forge and various workshops; a livery stable and a stone lock-up built by the army as well as the wood-built officers' quarters where the Viperines now lived. There was construction going on too. An extension was being added to the store and the men working on the roof wore ragged military uniforms which identified them as deserters. Post holes had been dug outside the saloon tent where someone was going to put up a sign. A parade of wagons was lined up in front of the store waiting to join the next train through.

Wesley was a stocky, round-faced man who smiled easily. He lacked that wiry appearance that so many of the men from the wagon trains had, dirt farmers making one last desperate bid to make a future for their families by taking the Emigrant Road. He had met many of them where the wagons gathered at Independence, Missouri. He found their determination humourless and their tired wives sour-faced; he rarely enjoyed their company.

Having done some buying and selling in New York in the past, Wesley understood the banter of making a deal and the necessity of keeping on good terms with a customer to win his trust. He knew that these skills would carry him far. He was also a practical man; repairing the wagon presented no problem to him. He was an optimist who believed he could make a success of anything.

A yellow-haired giant in a carpenter's apron rolled out of the saloon tent into the square, rocked back on his heels, blinked at the sunshine and started to walk away. Wesley hurried after him.

'Mister.'

The man turned, swaying slightly. Amusement lit his face as Wesley picked his way through the mud.

'You a carpenter?'

The man's laugh boomed like an echo.

'What do you think?'

'Just arrived,' Wesley said. 'Wagon's broke an axle. Name's Wesley Jackson.'

21

He held out his hand and the carpenter crushed it in his huge fist.

'Lars,' the man said. 'Everyone calls me The Norwegian.'

He gestured Wesley to follow.

The forge was a simple shack open to the air on one side. A fire smoldered beneath a hole in the roof and a bench was lined up against one wall. Different sized saws and various tools hung round the walls and the floor was ankle-deep in shavings. At the back of the shack was a bed frame with no mattress and a wooden chest. A coffee pot, a tin cup, a water jug and a plate and cutlery were piled on a table and a line of twine looped under the ceiling where Lars hung a blanket to separate his workplace from his living quarters. But for the moment, the blanket was folded and a mongrel dog slept on it beside the fire.

'Axle is more than a day's work,' Lars reflected. 'Ain't cheap.' He looked slyly at Wesley. 'Unless you got a mattress you want to trade.'

'I got one,' Wesley admitted. 'But it ain't for trade. My wife wouldn't want to sleep on bed wires.'

Lars sighed.

'Lucky man to have a wife and a mattress.'

Wesley nodded.

'I got a dog and no mattress,' Lars said sadly. He swayed slightly. 'And the dog's only got one eye.'

'How about I hire the workshop and do the work myself?' Wesley said.

Lars shrugged.

'Nine dollars a day for the hire.'

22

'Six,' Wesley said.

'You sure about the mattress?' Lars said.

'All right, seven dollars.'

Lars crushed Wesley's hand again.

'Start in the morning.'

'Know where I can get the wood?'

'I can get it. What do you want – pine, oak or elm?'

Wesley hesitated.

'Pine's cheap, oak's strong and elm's waterproof. Take your pick.' Then Lars added 'Oak's heaviest. You got strong oxen?'

'Ponies,' Wesley said. 'Two of 'em.'

'Best take pine. Pine's lightest. You're risking a break again but with two ponies you don't want no extra weight.'

Wesley agreed. 'How much?'

'Five dollars. Three if you take the wood and make it yourself.'

'I'll make it myself,' Wesley said.

Lars leaned forward and reached for Wesley's hand again.

'You can stay here tonight if you want,' Lars said. 'If you don't mind a bed with no mattress. Be glad of the company. One-Eye ain't much of a talker.'

'How come you got so many different types of wood out here?' Wesley said.

Lars laughed.

'You could call this busted axle country from the amount of business we do. Timber gets brought from the west. You decide to come back this way, you bring me a load.'

'Ain't never coming back,' Wesley said. 'You can count on that.'

Next morning Wesley was woken by a holla from Lars. The wire mesh of the unsprung bed pressed into his face, grey light filled the sky and the cold invaded his bones. The fire had died and the dog had gone. The big man was dragging a huge tree trunk across the square towards the carpenter's shop.

'Hey,' Lars called again.

Wesley levered himself off the bed and went to help.

'Here's your axle,' Lars said.

The pine trunk was almost three foot in diameter and over ten feet long. Wesley couldn't lift it on his own.

'Pay me five dollars now for the use of the shop,' Lars said. 'And buy me breakfast. Mick the Dog over at the saloon cooks up a feast of slapjacks and bacon. Might even have some eggs.'

Lars flung a bear-like arm round Wesley's shoulder and breathed last night's whiskey fumes into his face.

'I like you,' he said. 'We're gonna get along.'

The saloon tent was busy. Men sat at trestles shovelling back breakfast while a queue jostled at the counter. The air smelled of pork grease and coffee. By the time it got to Lars and Wesley's turn, the owner, who everyone knew as Mick the Dog, was in a foul mood. He was a heavy-set Irishman with a flushed, unshaven face. He relieved his temper by yelling orders at the Chinese cooks, visible through the back door of the tent, working at a griddle over an open fire.

'No bacon,' he barked before Lars could ask. 'Had three flitches brought up on the supply wagon from Independence yesterday. Some rogue had them away during the night.'

'Three?' Lars said. 'Someone setting up a restaurant?'

'Sell 'em to the Sioux. They'll trade their wives for hog meat,' Mick said. 'And you're too late for eggs, they're all gone.'

'Slapjacks is just fine.'

Mick yelled the order to the cooks and leaned conspiratorially over the trestle to Lars.

'Where's this so-called Viperine Militia? Supposed to be protecting us, ain't they? Supposed to be preventing all this thievery.'

Lars shrugged, letting Mick talk his anger out.

'I'll tell you,' Mick went on. 'They're out there like vultures preying on the wagons. Should be encouraging them to come into the fort so we can all do business. Place has gone to hell since the troopers pulled out.'

'Met 'em yesterday before the storm hit,' Wesley said. 'Told me I had to pay a charge. My wagon's a day's ride outside the post with a busted axle.'

'What did I tell you?' Mick slammed his fat hand down on the trestle. 'When the troopers were here folks could come and go as they pleased. What charge anyway?'

'Five dollars,' Wesley said. 'For the upkeep of the fort and protection by the militia.'

'You pay 'em?'

'Hell no.' Wesley hesitated. 'Me and my wife don't

25

aim to come into no trading posts if we can avoid it. We got our supplies and we're heading west as fast as we can. Wouldn't be here now if it wasn't for the axle.'

'There's another train due in tomorrow or the day after,' Mick said. 'They stick a protection charge on me every time a new train comes in on top of the rent. Those Viperines cheat the wagons and bleed the traders. Ain't no one safe.'

'Don't pay it,' Lars said matter-of-factly. 'I never pay a nickel to those snakes.'

'It's different for you,' Mick said. 'I got my daughter to worry about.'

Mick wiped his hands on his apron and changed the subject.

'Where's your wife?' He peered over Wesley's shoulder.

'Someone had to stay out with the wagon,' Wesley said briefly. 'We were part of a train out of Independence, a dozen wagons headed for California. But the others decided to take the fork for Oregon. Me and Eve always had our hearts set on California so we parted from them.'

Mick squinted at him as if he was trying to make up his mind about something.

'You went on alone?'

'A child died under the wheels of a wagon,' Wesley said. 'One day we made a nooning stop like always. Kid was playing underneath. Oxen moved and the kid. . . .'

Wesley spread his hands in explanation.

'I heard of that before,' Mick said. 'All kinds of things happen on the trail. When we came out my wife was pregnant. Smell of the sage made her sick. Day after day of it. That was the start of her illness.'

'Folks on the wagon train took it as a sign that they were on the wrong path,' Wesley said. 'Decided they weren't supposed to be heading for California so when the fork for Oregon came, they took that.'

'And you ended up here,' Mick said.

Wesley nodded.

'There's worse places,' Mick said. 'Just can't think of 'em.'

Mick's daughter, Dainty, a dirty-faced 6-year-old in a stained pinafore appeared balancing a plate of slapjacks in each hand and set them down on the end of a trestle. She took small, careful steps and was solemn with concentration. When Wesley and Lars had seated themselves, she tottered in with a tin mug of coffee in each hand.

The salt taste of the slapjacks stung their lips and the hot grease burned their mouths, but the food filled them up and gave them strength for the day.

'Know why they call him Mick the Dog?'

Lars' laughter spluttered through his mouthful of food.

'Last time somebody stole his flitches, he served up some strange tasting meat same time as a couple of mutts went missing. Claimed it was raccoon but nobody believed him.'

Lars leaned across Wesley and called out to Mick who was dealing with the next customer.

'Mick, you seen One-Eye this morning?'

Mick broke off from taking the order.

'Watch what you say in here, Lars,' Mick said darkly. 'This is my place.'

Lars laughed and shoved in another forkful which made the grease run down his chin.

After breakfast, Wesley returned to the workshop while Lars went off to join the men working on the extension to the store.

'If you can wait till tomorrow, I can give you a hand with the sawing,' Lars called. 'Take half the time.'

'Paid for the hire,' Wesley said. 'I'll do it.'

Wesley appraised the trunk and took the measure of Lars' tools. It was going to be a difficult job. Maybe he should wait another day and take up Lars' offer. A two-handed saw hung on the wall behind him. As he was considering how to start, he heard someone ride up to the workshop.

'Wesley?'

He looked round.

Eve smiled down at him.

'What are you doing here?'

3

Tolson's store smelled of new wood and coffee beans. Sacks of dry goods were stacked to the right of the door and to the left was a pyramid of bales of printed cotton with a few inches of the material pulled out to display the patterns. The owners, Frank and Ellie Tolson, stood at an oak-topped counter in front of high shelves packed with preserved foodstuffs, hardware, tools, work clothes and boxes of ammunition. The sound of hammering resounded through the building as the carpenters constructed another room to the side.

The Tolsons arrived at Fort Dove shortly after the Viperines claimed the land. They realized that as the territories opened up, the number of wagons along the Emigrant Road would increase year on year and there was money to be made. They agreed a ground rent with the Viperines and opened a store out of the back of their wagon.

Now Ma and Pa Tolson proudly stood in a wooden building, constructed for them and rented to them by the Viperines, which, although it was only a year old, was already being extended. Pa Tolson had established lines of supply with traders in Independence and had even begun to make contacts with importers in Boston with a view to stocking European goods. In fact, the bales of printed cotton at the front of the shop were direct from the mills of Lancashire, England.

All smiles, the Tolsons dealt efficiently with each customer. Unkempt children, told to stay outside by their parents, pressed their noses to the store window. A group of women from the wagons admired the prints near the door and a line of men queued at the counter for tobacco and ammunition. Stranger stood with them, waiting his turn. His frontiersman's jacket singled him out from the other men in their thin grey work shirts and while conversation rose and fell in the store, no one had the temerity to speak to him.

As Stranger approached the counter, two men shouldered past him and pushed in front. For a moment Pa Tolson was nonplussed. Should he insist on serving the customer at the head of the line or would it be easier to deal with Charles and Remy and get them out of the way? Looking past the insolent faces of the Viperine brothers, he met the untroubled gaze of Stranger who watched him to see what he would do.

'Now boys,' Tolson said. 'I believe this gentleman has been standing in line.'

Remy scratched his chin and stared around the store with exaggerated slowness. Charles snorted with laughter at his brother's pantomime.

'Don't see nobody,' Remy said innocently.

He stuck his thumbs inside his gun-belt, squared his

shoulders and continued his performance. Then his face hardened and he leaned over the counter.

'I want a tin of Bull Durham on account.'

'Now Remy, you know what we agreed,' Tolson said. He stepped a pace back from the counter. 'Landry was quite clear about that.'

The swell of happy conversation which had filled the store suddenly died. Brutal hammering battered the air as the carpenters working in the next room drove in their nails. The women who had been standing nearest the door slipped outside and towed their children away from the window. The men behind Stranger in the queue backed towards the edges of the room.

'I'm your landlord, Tolson,' Remy barked. 'I said a tin of Bull Durham.'

Ma Tolson pulled at her husband's sleeve and pressed a tin of tobacco into his hand.

Charles saw and snorted with laughter.

Stranger reached between the two men, seized their shoulders and shoved them apart. As they staggered, he turned, leaned against the counter and looked from one to the other.

'First is you owe me an apology, boys,' Stranger said. 'Pushed me aside like you didn't know I was there. Maybe you're shortsighted or just plain bad mannered. Either way, I'll let it pass if you're sorry. Second is, if the storekeeper don't want to sell you Bull Durham then you can't buy none—'

Ma Tolson screamed as the brothers launched themselves at Stranger. Stranger ducked their fists and dodged between them. With a carnivorous roar,

31

Charles dived at Stranger, grappled him round the waist and crashed him to the floor against the flour sacks. As Stranger tried to heave Charles aside, Remy lit into him with his boot. Two bone-cracking kicks caught Stranger in the ribs.

A scattergun blast made Remy hesitate before launching a third. Pa Tolson stood there with his shotgun pointed at the ceiling. He was scarlet faced and his eyes popped with fury. The carpenters who had been working in the adjoining room piled in through the door. Lars was ahead of them.

'You ain't fighting in my store,' Tolson yelled. 'I ain't having it.'

'Shut up, old man,' Remy spat. 'This ain't your business.'

As he took another kick at Stranger, Lars' huge forearm caught him round the throat and swung him off the ground. With his face suddenly the colour of raw liver, Remy scrabbled at Lars' huge arm. Charles pushed himself to his feet.

'Let him go, Lars,' Charles implored. 'We didn't mean nothing. Just a misunderstanding, that's all.'

Tolson lowered his shotgun and nodded to Lars.

Lars released his headlock and dumped Remy in a heap. Remy leapt to his feet, choking and clutching his throat. The brothers scrambled over each other to get to the door.

Remy stabbed a finger at Tolson. 'You ain't heard the last of this.'

Wincing with pain, Stranger picked himself up.

'And you.' Remy sounded as if wire was caught in his

32

throat. 'You ain't got no idea what can happen if you cross the Viperines.'

The brothers backed out through the door.

Lars took Stranger by the arm and hauled him upright.

'Easy,' Stranger said. He caught his breath. 'Been cattle kicked.'

'You come back with me,' Lars said. 'Got a place you can rest up.'

'What did you want, fella?' Tolson said.

'Came in to inquire the price of dry goods,' Stranger said. 'There's a wagon with a busted axle on the prairie. Folks lost their supplies in the storm.'

'You rest up a while.' Tolson smiled at him. 'We got everything you need when you're ready.' Then he added, 'That was a brave thing you did. Ain't many round here who will stand up to the Viperines. You best lay low for a while.'

Over at Lars' workshop, Eve brewed coffee on the fire.

'This is who I was telling you about,' she explained.

Wesley took Stranger's hand and started to thank him for calming the Appaloosa in the storm.

'Wasn't nothing.' Stranger shrugged.

He sat down heavily on the edge of the bed. Pain lined his face. Lars ran through what had happened at the store.

'Let me take a look,' Eve said. 'If you've busted a rib, you've got to have it bandaged up.'

Stranger protested but Eve was already easing his shoulder out of his buckskin jacket. Her fingers were so

33

efficient and light that he was hardly aware of what she was doing. He caught her eye as she freed his arm from the sleeve. She swiftly unbuttoned his cotton shirt. His ribs were tender with bruises. Her eye was caught by a small circular scar on the muscle of his arm, but she made no comment on it.

'Hurt when you cough?' Eve said.

Stranger cleared his throat.

'Don't reckon so.'

'That means your ribs are still in one piece. Just rest up a while and you'll be fine.'

'Those Viperine boys have got worse,' Lars said. 'When the troopers were here they had to be content with selling rotgut to the Sioux. Now they've taken over the post.'

'They're the ones rode out and said we'd have to pay this Militia Charge,' Eve said. 'They said everybody pays.'

'Sooner we get this axle made, sooner we can get out of here,' Wesley said.

'I'll help you,' Stranger said. 'You need a two-handed saw on that.'

Eve reached down and tore a strip from the hem of her petticoat, slipped the makeshift bandage round Stranger's rib cage and tied it tight. As she worked, Stranger fancied he saw a blush rise to her cheek.

'Finish your coffee,' Wesley said. 'Ain't no rush.' He turned to Eve. 'Sure he's up to this?'

'If he says so,' Eve said.

As Lars made his way back to work across the square, Wesley and Stranger heaved the pine up on to trestles.

Wesley cleaned off the small branches with a hand axe while Stranger levered the thick bark away with his bowie. Hanging amongst the tools, Wesley found a line looped round a nail beside a lump of blue chalk in a canvass bag. The line was dry and knotted in several places.

Wesley estimated the length of the axle, marked the ends with the point of his knife, chalked the line and handed one end to Stranger. With the line held taut a half inch away from the surface of the trunk, Wesley flicked it against the wood. In a tiny puff of chalk dust, a blue line appeared down the length of pine, straight and true.

Stranger took off his buckskin coat and Wesley passed him one end of the saw. The teeth were flaked with rust; it hadn't been sharpened for some time. Stranger faced Wesley across the huge pine. Each man steadied himself for a moment, then began. Seconds after the saw bit into the wood they found their rhythm. They continued regular sweeping strokes until pain burned their shoulders and sweat darkened the backs of their shirts. Neither wanted to be the first to quit. They glanced at each other over the top of the huge piece of wood, each of them serious-faced as they concentrated on maintaining the steady back-and-forth rhythm.

Eve watched them from inside the workshop. She had intended to make herself useful by tidying the place but Lars had so few possessions that this took her no time and she settled herself on the iron bedstead while the men worked. Wesley was the first to break a sweat. She cast her eyes over his strong, heavy-set shoulders. When she had sat beside him in the photographer's studio a few short weeks ago, thrilled and flattered by his offer of striking out west, with him sporting his best jacket and a new hat, she did not imagine he would be capable of tough work like this.

Stranger's buckskin jacket hung over the iron bed frame. Eve ran her eye over his tight, muscled arms. His body was lean and his movements were supple. There was no indication in his face that the work was causing him pain but she had seen the livid bruises on his ribs. He did not look at Wesley or her or what was around him, rather his grey eyes seemed to look inward, his concentration absorbed by the trance-like rhythm of the work.

Eventually, by an unspoken agreement signalled by some glance or inflection in the sawing movement, both men stepped back. They were barely halfway through the trunk and the blade was too hot to touch. A barrel stood inside the workshop and the men took turns helping themselves to scoops of water.

'Trimming the ends against the grain is the easy part,' Wesley said. 'We ain't got to cutting the length yet.'

'It's good wood,' Stranger said. 'Make a strong axle.'

While Stranger lifted the saw out of the cut and examined the teeth, Wesley sat down gratefully on the bed beside Eve.

'It'll need resharpening before we're done,' Stranger said.

The men worked through the afternoon. They

maintained the same steady pace and broke off at intervals to take scoops from the water butt. Bored with sitting still, Eve announced she was going to place an order for supplies at the store. She pulled her cotton bonnet close to her face and set off across the square. Bursts of hammering from Lars' carpentry work filled the air. Men and women from the wagons inspected the buildings, glad of something new to look at after hundreds of miles of empty prairie. Eve kept an eye out for the Viperines but there was no sign of them.

Ma Tolson welcomed Eve into the store and chatted to her over the bales of material. She complained how the noise of the building next door was driving her mad but enthused that it would be worth it in the end as the size of the store would double. She encouraged Eve to imagine herself wearing dresses run up from the new cotton prints and impressed her by explaining how the material was imported direct from Europe.

Eve liked all the patterns and could imagine herself wearing any of them. She wondered for a moment which one Wesley would like to see her in and which Stranger might choose for her. She pushed the thoughts away. She hadn't come here for cotton dresses: the rain had ruined their supplies and she felt guilty for that. At the same time, she was aware that Wesley had not raised a word of criticism against her even though it was her fault and replenishing their stocks here would be far more expensive than it had been in Independence.

She placed her order and told Ma Tolson that she would collect and settle up the following day. Outside, children scrambled and tussled around the wheels of the covered wagons; groups of men sat smoking their pipes outside the saloon tent; women chatted at the entrance to the store. The clang of iron being worked at the forge on the far side of the square chimed with Lars' belligerent hammering. The smell of wood smoke hung in the air, which meant that Mick had lit the fires at the back of the saloon tent in preparation for the evening cook-up.

Eve sauntered back to the carpentry shop. Wesley and Stranger were still working. Their pace had slowed and she sensed an unspoken competition between them in which whoever gave up first would lose. Wesley's expression was set in a grimace as sweat dripped from his brow and the colour had drained from Stranger's face. Eve smiled to herself.

'They've lit the cooking fires,' she said. 'We could eat soon.'

Both men simultaneously snapped away from their task as if she had broken a spell. Wesley snatched a scoop of water while Stranger sat down of the edge of the bedstead.

Lars joined the three of them at a trestle in the saloon tent and started to tell them about the carpentry problems he had overcome during the day. As they listened politely, Eve became aware that Dainty was peeping at her from the kitchen opening. As soon as Eve caught her eye, the little girl ducked back behind the canvas. Lars continued with his description of joists and joints as the smell of frying onions wafted into the tent from the cooking fires.

Men and women from the wagons began to fill up the tables and a crowd gathered at the bar. Eventually Mick appeared, served the customers' drinks and bellowed their food orders to the cooks. When there was no one left waiting, Mick stalked over to where Eve and the men were sitting. He nodded to each of them in turn. Lars started to ask him what the chow was that evening but Mick cut across him.

'Ain't no pretty way of saying this.' He looked straight at Stranger. 'Viperines say I ain't to serve you.'

His words hung in the air as they stared at him.

'Have to ask you to leave.'

'Which one said that?' Lars spluttered.

'Charles told me. Landry's orders.'

'Viperines own the land this saloon stands on,' Mick explained. 'Way I figure it, you're gonna be moving on in a day or two. I got to stay here. I'm sorry, fella.'

'The rest of us will order then,' Lars said. 'He can sit here if he don't order, can't he? We'll make like he ain't eating.'

Mick shook his head.

'Landry says I can't serve the rest of you if you're with him.'

'What do you say?' Stranger looked him in the eye.

'Mister, I ain't got no argument with you,' Mick explained. 'I got my daughter to think of.'

A few more men from the wagon train drifted in and waited by the bar.

'Got to get back to work,' Mick said. 'If the rest of you come back without him or if he leaves, I can serve you then.'

'Damn it, Mick.' Choking on his words, Lars jumped to his feet. 'I don't care what you say or the Viperines or nobody. You tell your cooks to plate us up some food and I'll collect it from round the back and take it to my shop.'

He gestured to the others to leave.

'Don't expect me to pay for it, neither.'

4

Back at the carpenter's shop Eve built up the fire. Lars had gone to collect the food from the kitchen behind the saloon tent. Stranger and Wesley inspected their handiwork. The ends of the axle had been cut clean and the trunk had been sawn in half. Three more sides waited to be shaped.

'Reckon I should move on,' Stranger said quietly. 'Less trouble if I wasn't around.'

Eve riddled the fire and watched the flames pop from the old ash.

'No,' Wesley said. 'You helped us, now we stick with you. We'll finish the axle in the morning. We'll hand axe the other three sides down for speed. Should be finished by midday.'

'What about the supplies?' Eve said.

'Take all we can carry on two horses. We'll walk alongside. Stranger can drag the axle behind his horse.'

'Might work,' Stranger reflected.

'Why shouldn't it?' Wesley said. 'If the Viperines come, we'll just tell 'em what we're doing. They'll see

41

we're moving out as fast as we can and leave us be.'

'What about this Militia Charge?' Stranger reminded him. 'That ain't just going to blow away in the wind.'

'We spent our money at Tolson's replacing supplies, ain't we? If we've already spent it we ain't got none left to pay a charge.'

Stranger ran his hand over the pine, crouched down and inspected the cleanness of the edge they had cut. Eve filled the coffee pot and stood it at the edge of the fire. The lid rattled as the water began to boil.

Shadows gathered in the corners of the square, between the buildings and under the wagons. Circles of orange light glowed through the roof of the saloon tent where Mick lit the oil lamps. The forge was silent and someone had pulled the doors of the livery stable closed for the night.

They all looked up when they heard the shot. There was a silence then shouts and the sound of running feet. A crowd forced its way out of the saloon tent and scattered towards the wagons. Stranger had already started across the square.

'Could be Lars,' Wesley called after him.

Stranger seemed not to hear. Wesley ran after him. As they neared the saloon, someone grabbed Wesley by the shoulder, a man from one of the wagons with terror in his voice.

'Don't go in there, mister. Turn right around.'

The man had run off before Wesley could ask him what had happened.

As Wesley followed close, Stranger slipped through the crowd and circled behind the saloon tent. Mick was there clasping Dainty tight to him. Smoke from the cooking fires curled round them. They stared down at Lars' huge body which lay face down in the dirt amidst smashed plates and scattered slapjacks. Stranger quickly knelt and checked for a pulse. After a few seconds, he looked up and shook his head.

'Lars was just collecting the food when Remy turned up,' Mick said. 'Must have followed him. You know what Lars is like. Mule-headed to the last. Remy tried to tell him he couldn't have nothing while you were with him. Lars told him to go to hell straight off. Remy shot him right where he stood.'

Mick hugged Dainty tighter.

'You see how it is round here,' Mick added. 'Take my advice and get out of here tonight. If you're gone before sunup, there's a chance they won't follow you.'

Stranger got to his feet.

'Get back to Eve,' he said.

'Where are you going?' Wesley said. 'If you're going after them, I'm with you.'

'Mick's right,' Stranger said. 'Viperines' blood is up. If we stay, there's gonna be more killing. Go back and saddle the horses.'

Stranger ducked round the side of the tent and was gone.

'Go,' Mick said. 'It ain't safe for nobody if you're here.'

Dusk deepened as Wesley hurried across the square. He could see Eve's silhouette crouched beside the fire at Lars' workshop. There was someone with her. He slowed his pace and peered through the gloom to make out who it was. He drew his colt: the thought gnawed at him that Remy or Charles had found her, but it was no one he recognized. He looked round for Stranger but there was no sign of him. He made his way to the side of the square and cut round the back of the buildings so as to approach unseen.

From behind the carpentry shop, Wesley was surprised to eavesdrop on friendly voices. Eve's laughter carried on the night air. The man spoke with a drunk's mild belligerence. He seemed to be insisting that he knew Eve from somewhere and would not believe her when she denied ever having met him. She was laughing to make light of his mistake as Wesley stepped into the circle of firelight.

'What do you want, mister?'

The man was unsteady on his feet.

'Just saw Constance from across the square,' the man grinned foolishly. 'Came over to exchange a greeting.'

'He thinks he recognizes me,' Eve said.

' 'Course I recognize you, Constance,' the man said. 'Ain't no mistaking you, what with that scar and all. Just don't understand why you say you don't know me.'

'My name is Eve Maddison, mister,' Eve said firmly. 'You have mistook me for somebody else.'

The man lurched and appealed to Wesley with a bemused smirk.

'Constance, ain't it? Plain as day.'

'You're mistaken mister,' Wesley said. 'The lady's told you.'

The man stumbled and made one last appeal.

'You know me Constance. It's me, Jack Bruford.'

Eve shook her head.

'Mister,' Wesley cut in. 'There's been a shooting. You can't stay here now.'

'All right.' Bruford raised his hands in mock surrender. 'I can see I ain't wanted.'

As he stepped unsteadily out into the square, he called over his shoulder.

'I don't know what game you're playing, Constance. Joe's on the train that gets here tomorrow. We'll see who you remember then.'

'So drunk he'd mistake his own mother,' Eve said.

'Don't matter right now,' Wesley said. 'Damp the fire. Everyone can see you from across the square. We got to saddle the horses and ride out right now. Lars has been shot.'

'Shot?'

Eve's mind was full of questions; she knew the answer to them all. Danger reared in the darkness. Fear scalpelled her belly.

'Where's Stranger?'

'My horse can haul the wood,' Wesley said. 'We'll take some of the tools and finish the axle out by the wagon. Hurry. The Viperines will be coming for us next.'

'Where's Stranger?'

Wesley heard the edge in her voice.

'Didn't say where he was going,' he said. 'Just hope he ain't looking for trouble.'

They worked quickly. Eve scooped water over the flames and the fire exploded in a hiss of steam. Wesley snatched together the tools he needed and hauled the saddles round the back of the building where the horses were tethered. As he worked, he explained to Eve what had happened. Eve helped him saddle up. Just as he was looping a rope round one end of the half-sawn trunk ready to tie it to his saddle, Stranger appeared with a sack of supplies over each shoulder.

'Got Pa Tolson to open up the store,' Stranger said. 'He had this put by for us.'

He roped one sack on to his saddle, the other on to Eve's.

As darkness thickened, they headed out.

They kept going all night. As the hours passed, clouds moved across the moon, sometimes laying bare a silver landscape in front of them, sometimes hiding it in pitch. The farther away from the fort they got, the harder the track was to recognize. They followed a path of trodden down sage and were guided by the instinct of the horses. Stranger and Wesley walked together; Eve followed.

During the first hour, Eve kept looking back expecting to see someone following; each sound in the brush or screech of an owl jolted her nerves. Her thoughts cartwheeled. Would the Viperines really let them go? And poor Lars – a kindly giant collecting supper. Could anyone get killed for less? As she walked, she rested her open palm on the neck of the Appaloosa; the hard power of his muscles, the toughness of his coat and the steadiness of his stride gave her strength.

Then there was Bruford. Loud-mouthed, drunken Jack Bruford who could ruin everything. Why hadn't

Wesley asked about him? Didn't he want to know why Bruford was so insistent that he knew her? Hadn't he realized it was obvious that he did?

Eve's mind went back to the afternoon she and Wesley met. She had arrived early at the Grapevine Coffee House and taken a table next to the window with a view of the street and the door. She carried the advertisement torn from the *News* in her purse; her heart was bursting. She wore her best bonnet and pulled her hair forward over her cheek to cover the scar.

Over the previous year, Eve had perfected the art of turning her face away from people as she spoke. Men often took this as a sign of demureness; sometimes she could hold a whole conversation without them noticing the white track and bulging flesh which disfigured her cheek. On this occasion she could not hope to keep her scar secret. The best she could hope for was that the man would not notice it right away and she had the chance to make some other first impression.

Eve knew Wesley was there to meet her as soon as she saw him. There was anxiety in his broad, handsome face as he surveyed the coffee house tables. His coat was brushed and she realized that he was wearing a new hat, obviously bought to impress her. This amused and flattered her and in that instant she believed that he might not reject her out of hand.

As Wesley leaned over and said her name, Eve forgot about demureness and turning away and the loop of hair which she had carefully pulled from under her bonnet. Hearing the voice of this man in a new hat startled her. She lifted her face and looked straight at him.

47

The swell of conversation which filled the room and the tinkle of cutlery against china faded away. She saw his eyes momentarily slide to the scar on her cheek.

'Eve Madison?'

His hand slipped her letter out of his jacket pocket and handed it to her.

'My name is Wesley Jackson.'

He rested his hand on the back of the chair opposite her.

'May I?'

The stiffness of the question told her he was nervous. Her heart flew; she was afraid she might laugh out loud. He had seen her scar and had still wanted to sit down. She tried to caution herself. Be careful. Don't rush. Let him speak. Let him ask. But her natural good nature broke through and she smiled. And he smiled back.

Wesley broke off his conversation with Stranger and hung back to let Eve catch up. Moonlight filled the prairie; it was still hours until dawn. Wesley held out his canteen for her. She took it gratefully and let the cool water wash down her throat.

'Doin' OK?' Wesley said.

An arc of shadow from the brim of his hat covered his face.

'How much longer, d'you reckon?'

'Five hours,' Wesley said. 'Four if we keep up this pace.'

'I was thinking about the Grapevine,' Eve said. 'First time I saw you.'

Wesley laughed. 'Didn't mention nothing about

busted axles in the newspaper. You didn't sign up for this.'

'What did you think?' she said, 'First time you saw me.'

Wesley laughed again.

'Fishin' for a compliment?'

'I know it sounds like that but I ain't. I just want you to answer the question.'

'Guess I thought there's a fine lookin' woman, better check to see if she's Miss Madison or I'll be taking the wrong one to California.'

There was amusement in his voice.

'You didn't think—'

'What?'

'About the scar—'

Wesley paused.

'What about it? Everyone carries a scar or two. Some you can see, some you can't. Just means something happened in the past and now it's healed over and done with. No point worrying about it. You've got to concentrate on what's up ahead.'

Dry, bitter perfume filled the night air as they trod through the sage. The moon dipped behind a cloud again and Eve patted the neck of the Appaloosa.

'What happens if something from the past comes up into the future?' she said.

Eve sensed Wesley was staring at her through the darkness.

'You deal with it when it comes.'

'Look,' Stranger called.

Up ahead, early dawn light thinned the darkness.

Silhouetted on the far horizon was a circle of wagons.

'Ain't too far from where we're headed,' Stranger said. 'Reckon they'll move into Fort Dove as soon as it gets light.'

'Will they pass by us?' Eve said.

'Reckon they will. We should give them a warning about the Viperines.'

Ten wagons, twelve, it was impossible to say how many there were from here. Eve strained her eyes and tried to count. The moon dipped behind a cloud again. Only the first faint smudge of dawn remained.

'Wes,' she said. 'There's something I've got to tell you.'

Wesley put his finger to his lips.

'No need to tell me anything.' He smiled at her. 'I know everything I need to for now. The rest I can guess at.'

5

Stranger had expected the wagons to move off at dawn but they sat on the horizon long after morning light flooded the sky. Why hadn't they broken the circle? An hour later, as Stranger, Wesley and Eve approached the train, they realized that the horses were hobbled and the people were keeping out of sight.

By nine o'clock the air was warm and the sky was wide and empty. A line of wood smoke rose straight up from the fire in the middle of the wagons. Stranger hollered a greeting from fifty yards off.

A rifle shot cracked and the bullet sang through the air. A warning shot. Someone called out from the wagons but they couldn't make out the words. Stranger handed Wesley the reins to his horse.

'You ain't going in there?' Wesley said.

Stranger had raised his hands high above his head and strode forward. The voice from the wagon shouted something again. Stranger undid his gun belt and let it fall to the ground but did not slacken his pace. Wesley and Eve held their breath and watched.

A man holding an old Sharps hunting rifle stepped out from behind a wagon and faced Stranger. A farmer. His face was thin under his misshapen hat and his faded shirt was patched.

'You from the fort?'

'Come from there,' Stranger said. 'Folks I'm with have got a wagon with a busted axle.'

'Went in for supplies?' the man said.

'Supplies got ruined in the storm. Had to replace them. Dragged the wood out to make a new axle.'

'Who's them two with you?'

Stranger paused.

'You're asking a lot of questions, friend.'

The man's eyes hardened as he raised the barrel of the Sharps and pointed it at Stranger's chest.

'The folks who own the wagon,' Stranger said patiently.

The rifle barrel twitched again.

'I was headed east and chanced upon 'em.'

'Sure you ain't from the fort?' the man said.

Stranger lowered his hands.

'I'm sure.'

The man lowered his rifle.

'Henry Winter,' the man said and held out his hand to Stranger. 'Had some trouble yesterday. Three guys rode up and told us we had to pay a charge in support of their militia. Folks on this train scraped together every last nickel they had to make this journey and they ain't got none to spare.'

Stranger nodded. Men began to climb out of their wagons; none of them carried a weapon.

'One of the guys starts arguing with them,' Winter went on. 'Two of them beat him real bad. The third one grabs one of the women and holds a pistol to her head to make sure nobody intervenes.'

'Viperine brothers,' Stranger said. 'Last night they shot a man who was helping us. We left to make sure there was no more killing.'

'Near out of supplies. We need to go into the fort,' Winter said. 'Ain't got the money to pay a Militia Charge. We were debating what to do when you happened along.'

A group of men stood round Stranger. Women began to climb out of the wagons.

'Hurt the man bad?' Stranger said.

'Joe? He'll live. Resting up in one of the wagons.' Winter lowered his voice. 'Came across him in Independence just as we were starting out. Said his wife had run off and left him. He was in a pitiful state, drinkin' and feeling sorry for himself. We took a vote and decided to let him travel with us provided he quit the bottle. Turns out he's a real hothead. If someone's gonna lose his temper, it's gonna be Joe.'

'Next trading post is a hundred miles,' Stranger said.

Winter looked grim.

'Hundred miles is eight days for us, more likely nine. We got supplies for two at the outside.'

'You and those folks out there,' Winter said. 'If we all stuck together . . .'

'Face down the Viperines?' Stranger said.

Winter nodded. Stranger waved to Wesley and Eve to come into the circle of wagons. They stood where he had left them holding the horses, fifty yards off.

'Could be that the Viperines come out here again,' Stranger said. 'We slipped away in the night. They'll have found that out by now and they won't like it. It'll be me they want first.'

The onlookers began to talk intently amongst themselves and turned away from Stranger so he could not hear their words.

'First thing I got to do is get this axle fixed,' Stranger said. 'Said I'd do that.'

'We can help you,' Henry said.

Stranger looked over to Eve and Wesley. Neither of them had moved. He waved to them again. With a glance at Winter, he strode over to collect his gun belt from where he had let it fall midway between the circle of wagons and where Eve and Wesley stood. Again Stranger gestured to them to approach and when they did not, he strode towards them.

'Eve ain't keen on going into the train,' Wesley said. 'Reckon we'll walk on to our wagon.'

'They've offered to fix the axle,' Stranger said. 'Seem like regular folks.'

He went on to tell them about the Viperines' visit to the wagons.

'Beat a guy up pretty bad,' Stranger said. 'If the Viperines come out here again they ain't got a chance. They ain't got hardly any food left. If they don't make it in to the store, some of 'em will starve.'

Stranger looked at Eve.

'Reckon the womenfolk would like to talk to you. Anyhow, best that we stick together.'

Eve pulled her cotton bonnet down to hide her face and looked away. Stranger took the reins to his horse and began to lead it back towards the wagons.

The men were glad to have something to take their minds off the Viperines and fell on Wesley's half-made axle. They walked round it, ran their hands over it, appraised the strength of the grain and admired the straightness of the cut. They brushed aside Wesley's suggestions that it would be quicker to use axes and produced saws and trestles from their wagons, marked out guidelines and set about the trunk. Wesley was amongst them ready to advise and comment but the men were used to working together and had no need of direction.

Eve hung back in the crowd of womenfolk, said little and pulled her bonnet down. Stranger and Henry Winter stood at the edge of the circle of wagons and kept lookout for the Viperines.

An hour passed. While two men sawed, two others sharpened and oiled another saw. When it was ready they exchanged. At the same time two other men would take over the sawing. Working in a team like this, they cut the same quantity of wood in an hour that Stranger and Wesley using Lars' old blade had managed in a morning. As the heat of the day rose to its height, the men completed the work.

Having roped the finished axle to Wesley's horse, the men from the wagons insisted on riding out with him. Despite their protestations, Eve untied a sack of flour from her horse and handed it to the women. For a brief moment, everyone forgot about the Viperines. Stranger and Wesley admired the workmanship of the axle; the women were profuse in their thanks for flour. They embraced Eve in turn, kissed her and wished her well. She climbed on her horse, her face flushed, surprised and grateful for the feeling of goodwill.

No one paid attention to a man who let himself down from one of the wagons, tousle-haired as if he had been sleeping, apparently disturbed by the noise. His face was bruised and his movements were stiff. He watched the send-off but took no part in it. He studied Wesley and Stranger for a moment and then his eye rested on Eve. He barged through the crowd and reached up and seized her wrist. Before anyone realized what was happening he hauled her down from her horse. Her foot caught in the stirrup and she screamed with shock and pain. Men in the crowd shouted. Those nearest tried to grab him but the man shook them off. He was yelling, his face twisted with fury.

Wesley leapt down off his horse and grabbed the man's arm. The man socked him with a vicious left, a fighter's punch. The crowd shrank back as Wesley reeled.

Eve, her ankle free from the stirrup, scrambled to her feet with the man's grip still locked on to her wrist. She bombarded him with punches and hacked at his shins. The man held her at arm's length.

'You know me,' Joe yelled to the crowd. 'You know my story. Well, this is her. This is the one that ruined me. This is my wife, Constance Briarly.'

The crowd gasped.

56

'The one that ran off, like I told you. Looks like she hitched up with another man, joined him in his wagon and headed west, just like we planned to do.'

The oiled, metallic snick of a colt being cocked cut through his words. Wesley levered himself to his feet, his gun trained on Joe.

'Let her go.'

'What are you gonna do?' Joe leered. 'Shoot an unarmed man in front of these hymn singers?'

'She's with me,' Wesley said. 'Her name's Eve.'

There was whispering in the crowd as if no one could make up their mind. Stranger took a pace forward. Eve struggled and Joe ratcheted his grip tighter.

'Point that gun at me all you want,' Joe said. 'What I say is right. I got a wedding licence to prove it. You expect me to let my wife run off?'

'You're pushing your luck, mister,' Wesley said. 'I'm close to blowing your head off.'

'See.' Joe appealed to the crowd. 'You're good people. You can see what I'm up against. This man's took my wife off me by force and now he's threatening to shoot me.'

The crowd turned to each other in a storm of discussion. Wesley took a step nearer Joe, his gun still raised. Joe jerked Eve in front of him as a shield, twisted her arm behind her back with one hand and held her with his other arm round her throat. In the struggle Eve's bonnet was pushed back off her head and the scar, which ran in an arc from the corner of her eye to the edge of her mouth, was plain for everyone to see. The crowd gasped. One woman stifled a scream. Some of the men appealed to Joe but he ignored them. Each time Eve struggled, Joe levered her arm until the sinews cracked.

Stranger pushed through the crowd.

'We've heard what you two fellas have to say but we ain't heard from the person in the middle of all this.' He nodded to Wesley. 'You holster your gun.' He turned to Joe. 'You let her go. Then we'll hear her speak.'

Wesley slid his gun back into his holster but kept his eyes fixed on Joe. Joe released his grip on Eve.

'What Joe says is true,' Eve began. 'But the way he tells it ain't.' She searched the faces in the crowd. The women in their cotton bonnets and the thin-faced men lined up like a jury.

'I am married to Joe,' Eve said. 'I ran off and left him. I answered an advertisement in the *New York News* from a man who wanted a partner on the trail. We intended to start a new life.'

'See?' Joe yelled. 'I was telling the truth. This here's my wife and she ran off from me and took up with another man by her own admission. I mean to take her back right here and now. I guess by rights I should shoot him too, but I won't do that because of the spirit of forgiveness that you folks have taught me.'

The crowd shifted uneasily.

'Wesley didn't know,' Eve went on. 'I said I was a widow woman.'

Joe roared in triumph. 'See what kind of wife I got? Even lies to the person she runs off with.'

Wesley's hands clenched into fists.

'All we wanted was the chance of a new life out west,' Eve said. 'It's what all of us wants, ain't it?'

Henry's voice thundered over the heads of them all.

'Why did you run off from your husband? Tell us that.'

Eve turned to face him.

'I left my husband because he was a drunk and he used to beat on me. I reasoned with him but it didn't do no good. Every time he sobered up, he'd say how sorry he was and how he never meant to harm me and then next time he got drunk, he'd do it over again. Had this feeling that one day, whether he meant to or not, he might kill me.'

'She's lyin',' Joe howled. 'There ain't no proof. She's my wife and she ran off. That's the only facts there is.'

'See this scar,' Eve continued calmly. 'Up to this minute, I was ashamed. I hid my face. I looked to one side when people spoke to me. I never went places. I'm used to folks who look away and others who stare like they've never seen anything so ugly.'

Eve turned to show everyone in the crowd.

'First time I met Wesley, he saw it. Didn't even blink. He asked me straight off to come out to California with him. He's a good man. He don't stand in judgement and he ain't interested in what's past.'

'This is my wife,' Joe yelled. 'Remember that, while you're listenin' to her stories.'

'Know who put this scar there?' Eve stared from face to face and gave them a chance to reply.

'Joe did. My husband.'

No one spoke. There was just the rustle of the breeze

59

moving though the sagebrush, the occasional stamp of one of the horses and the jingle of a harness.

'One night I told him I was going to leave,' Eve said quietly. 'Told him I wanted a new life. Told him everyone deserves the chance of happiness.'

Eve stared at the ground. The boldness with which she had started speaking deserted her and her voice faded.

'He took up a bottle, broke it and said he was going to make sure no one ever wanted me.'

Then Eve rallied herself again. She looked into the crowd and finally at Stranger and she spoke clearly.

'I ran off that same night.'

'It was a mistake,' Joe said. 'I got a temper, I'll admit that. My wife said she was leaving me. I lashed out. It wasn't no deliberate thing. It wasn't planned.'

He stared contemptuously round but the faces of the crowd were closed against him.

'I fought the Viperines for you yesterday. I didn't stand about watching like the rest of you. Me and my temper was useful to you then. If a few of you men had joined in with me then we would have seen off them Viperine boys and wouldn't have the trouble we got now.'

'Shut up,' Stranger said. 'You said your piece.'

He looked at Eve.

'Everyone should have a chance at happiness, you're right. And that's surely something you got to make for yourself.'

'She's my wife,' Joe yelled. 'She stays with me. The law says so.'

'This is the frontier,' Stranger said. 'There ain't no law here; there ain't no rules and regulations. There's just people. Some of 'em try to do what's right and some of 'em don't pay no mind to that.'

'See what he's doing?' Joe screamed, turning from one onlooker to another. 'Taking away a man's legal wife.'

'We'll ride out and fix the axle now,' Stranger said. 'Any of you folks from the train wants to help us get the job done faster, we'd appreciate it.'

Then he turned to Joe and swung a hammer punch which cracked the side of his jaw and sent him sprawling amongst the sage.

'This ain't over,' Joe spluttered through a mouthful of blood. 'I'll come for you and I'll get her back.' He pointed his finger impotently after them as they rode out but did not get to his feet until they had gone.

The six men who had worked on the axle rode out with Stranger and the others. Within an hour they expected their wagon to come into view but there was no sign of it. When they arrived at a place where a rectangle of sagebrush was trodden down, Wesley climbed out of his saddle.

'This is where we left it,' he said. 'Here's the rock that busted the axle.'

Incredible. Wesley walked around the empty space with his hat pushed back on his head.

'Disappeared into thin air,' Wesley said.

'Here's your answer,' Stranger said suddenly.

Three riders were approaching from the direction of

the wagon train. Wesley slid his pistol out of its holster.

'Could take 'em down while they're still riding.'

'Put your gun away,' Stranger said. 'They ain't come to shoot us.'

The Viperine brothers rode up close. They reined in their horses and leaned forward in their saddles.

'Done you a favour,' Remy said. 'Got some of our boys to take an axle off an old wagon back at the fort and fit it on yours.'

A smirk danced on his mouth.

'Thought we were all bad, didn't you?' Charles said. 'If you'd have come to us instead of that oaf Lars you could have left here yesterday.'

' 'Course,' Remy said. 'We had to take your wagon back to the fort because you ain't paid the charge.'

'What?' Wesley said.

'Wagon's forfeit till you pay the Militia Charge,' Landry snarled. 'And there's something else. We just come from the wagon train. Man there says you fellas have kidnapped his wife. Even if the guy is a loud-mouth, that's a serious charge. Can't let that pass now, can we?' Landry looked at Stranger. 'I know you'd want to do what's right.'

'Do I look like I'm kidnapped?' Eve snapped.

'Cover your face,' Landry sneered. 'That scar ain't sightly.'

Remy and Charles grinned as though this was a game and they had the upper hand. But not Landry. His face was expressionless and his eyes were hard.

'We'll be turning back to the fort now. That wagon train is heading in too. They got the mail and New York newspapers to deliver so that reduces their charge. But yours just keeps on growing. There's the Milita Charge, the fee for reclaiming the wagon and the cost of fitting the axle. If this woman really is that fella's wife, kidnapping means a spell in the lock-up.'

Landry wheeled his horse and the others followed.

'And don't think about shooting us in the back,' he called over his shoulder. 'If we ain't returned by evening, my boys are instructed to use your wagon as kindling.'

6

Leaden afternoon heat weighed on the prairie and the sage smelled bitter as Stranger and the others loaded the axle into Henry Winter's wagon. Winter tried to persuade Stranger to hang back and ride with the train so they could all face the Viperines together.

'Had a meeting,' Winter said. 'Folks decided that we got to strike a deal. We don't want violence.'

Stranger listened patiently.

'Worked out well.' Winter forced a smile. 'When they heard we was carrying the mail, they gave us a reduction in the charge. We ain't got money to pay so the men agreed to do building work as payment.'

'How much work?'

'Ten men for a week.'

Stranger said nothing.

'Didn't have no choice,' Winter continued. 'At least we can rest the animals.'

'Think you've talked the train out of trouble?'

'Sure you won't ride with us?' Winter said.

'Appreciate your position,' Stranger said. 'But I ain't

about to negotiate with the Viperines.'

'You'll put those other folks in danger,' Winter said.

'There's always danger,' Stranger said. 'If they decide to ride with me, that's their choice.'

He turned his horse to where Eve and Wesley waited for him.

Light was dying by the time they rode into the fort. Just like before, there were wagons drawn up round the square, a column of smoke rose from the fires behind the saloon tent and children chased each other between the buildings. One thing was different though: the sign over the doorway to the store which carried Tolson's name had been taken down.

'Wagon ain't here,' Wesley said. 'Reckon they've hidden it?'

Stranger scanned the square.

'Why would they do that?'

'Could try the livery,' Eve said.

The livery stable was set back off the square. Its weather-bleached façade showed it was one of the oldest buildings. The faded sign over the door declared 'Viperine's Livery. Feed and Water Always Available'. The doors were open and the place was empty. Stranger dismounted and led his horse inside. Wesley rode round behind the building while Eve waited.

A second later there was a shout from Wesley; the others hurried to join him. Leaning at a crazy angle behind the building was their wagon. The two back wheels and an axle they did not recognize lay beside it. Wesley climbed inside.

'Looks like a twister passed through,' he shouted.

'Can't tell if any thing's missing.'

'Train will be here tomorrow,' Stranger said. 'We can fix the new axle and leave by the afternoon.'

'Reckon the Viperines will let us leave?' Wesley said. 'If we don't pay their damn charge we'll make a whole heap of trouble for ourselves.'

'They're the one's making trouble, not us,' Stranger said. 'Trouble's what we're trying to stay away from.'

'Maybe we should pay,' Wesley said. 'Cut a deal like Henry Winter did.'

'Too late,' Eve said. 'We start trying to negotiate now, Viperines are just gonna put the price up. Winter's already given them ten men for a week. Who's to say they won't dream up another charge when the week is up?'

'We could leave the wagon,' Wesley said. 'Just ride out with what we can carry. We'll meet up with another train along the trail. They'd take us in.'

'Everything we own is in that wagon,' Eve said. 'You gonna let the Viperines take it from us?'

'I'll see if I can find some feed for the horses,' Stranger said. He took the reins of the three horses and led them into the stable.

Eve climbed into the wagon and brought out the framed letter, photograph and cutting. The glass had been cracked under some Viperine boot heel.

'It's still here,' she said. 'Gonna hang this on our cabin wall when we get to California.'

'Kinda guessed you were running from someone,' Wesley said.

'Thought you wouldn't take me with you if I told you I already had a husband.'

'Would have, if you'd told me what he did,' Wesley said. 'No mistake about that.'

Eve ran the tips of her fingers along the scar on her face.

'Joe ain't gonna let this lie,' Eve said.

'You still want to come to California?' Wesley said.

Eve laughed. 'You know I do.'

'Then if he comes for me, I'll be ready for him.'

'Joe's a rattlesnake. He's got Winter's people to take him in right now. Next thing you know he'll be selling them out to the Viperines. He's got a way of making people believe in him and then he turns on them.'

'How come you took up with a man like that?'

'He's persuasive,' Eve said. 'I was alone.'

Wesley nodded.

'You don't understand,' she went on. 'A woman ain't got no freedom: she can't go no place, can't own nothing. I'd heard it was a better life for women in the west, more equal. I'd heard women even owned land out there. When I saw your advertisement and it said "companion wanted", I thought that sounds about as equal as it's going to get. I thought it must have been a nice fella put that in the *New York News*.'

Eve laughed.

' 'Course, I ain't always right.'

She ducked back as Wesley made a playful lunge at her.

'You stood up for me,' Eve said. 'Against Joe. I thought you were going to shoot him.'

'Didn't have a clear shot,' Wesley said. His face darkened.

67

'No one's done that for me before,' Eve said. 'Anyhow, I never considered you a gunman.'

'Joe ain't no threat compared to the Viperines,' Wesley said. 'I ain't sure Stranger realizes what a nest of snakes this fort is.'

'He knows,' Eve said. 'He just don't show it.'

Wesley raided the log pile behind the stable to shore up the base of the wagon and inspected the woodwork for signs of damage. As soon as this was done, he crawled underneath, ran his hand over every inch of the underside and when he was satisfied, turned his attention to the neck yoke.

'Might as well make use of the time we got,' he called to Eve.

Eve climbed up into the wagon to make some order out of their heap of possessions.

'Stranger tell you where he was headed?' Wesley called as he worked.

'East,' Eve said.

'Where did he come from?'

'Didn't ask him.'

'Unusual, ain't it? Everyone heading west and Stranger's going in the opposite direction.'

'Must have a reason,' Eve said.

Wesley methodically worked his way over the wagon's falling tongue, which extended out to the yoke and checked for the slightest sign of a split in the wood. But the grain had been chosen for strength, crafted by the builder and polished smooth by the backs of the horses. A circle of rust surrounded each of the iron bolts which fixed the tongue to the trees at the front of the wagon, but the bolts held good and the trees allowed proper movement. Next he walked round the wagon to check the bonnet fixings. Eve climbed down from the wagon and watched the thorough, careful way he studied each one in turn.

'If Joe does come . . .' she began.

'He will,' Wesley said. 'When he does, we've just got to keep calm around him. He gets dangerous when he flies off into a rage.'

Wesley smiled at her.

'He don't really want me,' Eve confessed. 'Just wants to show folks he can stop me getting away. Anyhow, whatever he says or does, I ain't never going back with him. That's for sure.'

'Thinks we made him look foolish,' Wesley said. 'While he's got that idea in his head, we got to be careful. When the train gets here, you stick close to me.'

'I know you're a man I can tie to, Wes, I've always known that,' Eve said. 'But I should have a gun, same as you. Joe and the Viperines are looking for trouble with me as well as you.'

'Less likely to get shot at if you ain't packin',' Wesley said. 'Could say it's safer not to carry.'

'Don't feel safer,' Eve said. 'Feels like you're inviting trouble in.'

Wesley looked up from where he had been inspecting the hinges on the backboard.

A riderless horse ambled up the side of the stable to where they were talking. Stranger's bay. It carried no saddle and the reins hung down over its head. The horse whinnied to show it recognized them. Eve smoothed his neck and spoke into his ear as she looped the reins over a hook on the side of the wagon. Wesley slid his colt out of its holster.

'Hear anything?'

Eve shook her head. Wesley beckoned her to follow and they hurried down the side of the stable. Eve's Appaloosa and Wesley's horse stood saddled and untethered a few yards outside the stable door. Wesley grasped Eve's arm to stop her running out to them. He scanned the square. Nothing unusual. A gang of children played round the wagons; a group of women stood outside the store.

Wesley nodded to Eve to stay where she was while he slipped into the stable. As the shadows swallowed him, she stepped out and called softly to the horses. The Appaloosa nickered and began to walk towards her; Wesley's horse followed. Eve gathered up both sets of reins and led them round the side of the stable to wait. She could hear Wesley's cautious footsteps inside and the creak of the ladder as he climbed up into the hayloft. When he appeared at the door again, he shook his head.

'No sign of him,' he said. 'His saddle is in the middle of the floor.'

Wesley holstered his gun.

'Plenty of empty stalls. We'll see to the horses.'

As they fed and watered the animals, they both kept glancing towards the open doors and listened out for the sound of a footstep. Nothing. Outside they could hear the children's laughter as they chased each other round the wagons and snatches of conversation as people passed by in the direction of the saloon tent.

When they finished, they headed out to the square. Eve's eye was caught by a glint of metal in the straw by the stable door. She caught her breath. Stranger's gun belt with the new Starr pistols still in the holsters lay as if he had dropped it where he stood. Eve gathered it up. Wesley's gun was in his hand again and he peered into the shadows.

'Must have jumped him,' Wesley said. 'Three against one.'

'What do they want with him anyway?' Eve said.

Wesley flicked open the chamber of his gun and checked the shells.

'Took a dislike to him the first time they saw him.'

Eve removed one of the Starrs from the belt. She kicked aside the straw and buried the belt and the second gun.

'What are you doing?' Wesley said. 'You can't use that.'

The handle of the gun felt smooth and comfortable in Eve's hand and the weight was balanced and true. She took off her cotton bonnet and disguised the gun with it.

'Lighter than I thought,' she said.

'Viperines see you with a gun, they'll shoot you right off. Why don't you stay with the horses and let me look for Stranger?'

'We should stick together,' Eve said. 'Ain't that what you said?'

Side by side, they stepped out of the livery stable into the grey dusk.

7

Remy Viperine was waiting for them. As Wesley, then Eve, emerged into the square, Remy slid round the corner of the stable.

'Hey,' he called softly.

As they turned, Charles appeared at the opposite corner. Remy leaned indolently against the wall. A straw stuck out of the side of his mouth; his thumbs were tucked into his gun belt. Wesley's hand flew to his holster and then hesitated. Charles leveled a shotgun at Eve. Eve still held the pistol disguised by her cotton bonnet. Close by, children scrambled about under the wagons laughing and calling to each other.

Remy saw Wesley's hand hover over his gun.

'No need for that. I got some information for you.'

He spoke encouragingly, as if Wesley would be pleased at what he had to say.

'I'm listenin',' Wesley said.

Eve felt the easy balance of the Starr in her hand. She heard Charles breathing behind her. She couldn't tell whether he knew she was holding a gun.

'Your friend,' Remy began. 'The one that's all done up like a frontiersman from the old days.'

'I know who you mean,' Wesley snapped.

'Well, he broke the law.' Wesley paused. 'And that's a serious matter.'

Remy's eyes narrowed as he waited for Wesley's reaction.

'Got himself arrested by the Militia.' He paused again. 'That's us.' He rolled the straw to the other side of his mouth. A smile flickered on his lips.

Eve heard Charles snort with laughter behind her.

'On a murder charge,' Remy went on. 'He's locked up right now on Landry's orders.'

'What?' Wesley said.

'Shot old Lars the Norwegian stone dead.'

Wesley stiffened.

'That's a cold-hearted lie and you know it.'

'Got a witness who was right there and saw him do it.'

'Bull,' Wesley said. 'What witness?'

'Lars was shot right behind the saloon tent in front of the cooking fires. Mick the Dog saw the whole thing.'

Remy prised himself off the wall and stood upright, his thumbs still hooked in his belt.

'Mick is an upstanding member of this community,' Remy said. 'He ain't some wagon train drifter chasing a pipe dream in California. He's raising his family right here. Couldn't get a more reliable witness.'

Wesley's hand hovered over his gun again; Remy's eyes followed it.

'If the troopers were here,' Remy went on, 'your friend would be hanging from a gallows right now.

74

Guess Landry is gonna have us shoot 'im.'

Remy spat the straw from his mouth and leaned forward.

'Know whose fault this is?' he said. His eyes bored into Wesley. 'Yours, my friend. If you'd paid the Militia Charge like we asked, you could have fixed your wagon and gone on your way. None of this would have happened.'

'There ain't no such thing as a Militia Charge,' Wesley said. 'This is a free country.'

'There's a charge if we say there is,' Remy said. 'Reason is, there's a price on everything. Just look around you. You see guys shooting at each other? You see drunk fellas brawling in the streets? Outside the fort, you see Sioux on the rampage? No you don't. And you know why that is?'

Remy stared into Wesley's eyes.

'It's because people are afraid. They're afraid of the Viperines. They're afraid of me and my brothers. That's what makes the law around here. That's what keeps the peace. And if we say we raise a charge for protecting Fort Dove, then that's what we do.'

Wesley squared up to him. He folded his arms over his chest and stared defiantly back.

'You're a liar. Stranger never killed nobody. And just because folks round here is scared of you, don't mean you're protecting them from nothing.'

Remy's hands tightened into fists until the knuckles were white. His eyes narrowed and his mouth was a slit.

'In the morning,' Remy spat, 'when we've dealt with this Stranger, when the new wagon train is here, when you've fixed your wagon and when you've paid your Militia Charge, then you can be on your way.'

Anger burned in Remy's face. Eve lightly took hold of Wesley's wrist.

'We're going over to the saloon,' Eve said quietly. 'Reckon we've both learned a lot from the information you've given us.'

With the Starr feeling cool in her hand, Eve led Wesley across the square and left Remy and Charles to stare after them.

At the entrance to the saloon tent, Wesley turned. He had a clear view of the entrance to the livery stable. The Viperines had disappeared. Wesley and Eve glanced at each other and hurried round the tent and across the open ground to the lock-up.

The red stone walls were solid and the iron door was locked fast. A barred window was let high into the side wall. Stranger answered Wesley's call.

'Two of them jumped me,' Stranger said. 'Dragged me in here.'

'You hurt?' Eve said.

'I'm OK,' Stranger said.

'I got your gun. I can pass it to you.'

Stranger's hand appeared through the bars. Wesley hoisted Eve up by the waist.

'Soon as they unlock this door, you come out blazing,' Wesley said.

'Don't you hang around here now,' Stranger said. 'They're liable to come and check on me.'

'I'll get you some food from the saloon,' Eve said. 'You hungry?'

76

'Can't remember the last time I ate,' Stranger said.

As usual, in the saloon tent, Mick was shouting orders to his cooks. He stepped back from the trestle as Wesley and Eve approached.

'We want a plate to take to the lock-up,' Wesley said. 'And a bottle of water.'

Mick looked away from them and shouted the order through the gap in the tent.

'Didn't think I'd be seeing you again,' Mick said cautiously.

'Hear you're a witness,' Wesley said.

'So?'

'Why would you identify the wrong guy?'

Mick's sweaty face was the colour of paste.

'Viperines own this place,' Mick said. 'I got to look after my girl.'

The little almond-faced girl in a dirty pinafore carried out a plate of eggs and slapjacks and a tin mug of water and set them down in front of her father. Without speaking, she disappeared back to the kitchen.

'That's Dainty,' Mick said. 'Six years old. Know what the Viperines would do to her if I cross them?'

'She's a child,' Wesley said.

'They'd sell her,' Mick said. 'For every wagon load of people that passes through here holding Bibles, there's one which is full of the meanest lowlifes you can imagine. It's like the country is on a tilt and every now and then the New York sewers empty into the West.'

Mick twisted his apron in his hands. Sweat stood out on his forehead and his face was grey.

'You said you saw who shot Lars,' Wesley said.

'What's this guy to me?' Mick said. 'Some drifter riding around the frontier. There's guys like him all over. They don't amount to nothing. They stay in one place a week and then they're gone.'

'You're wrong about him,' Wesley said. 'And he's in the lock-up right now because of your say so.'

'You think the Viperines locked him up because of me?' Mick gave a bitter laugh. 'If they want to lock him up, they lock him up. If they want to shoot him, they shoot him. What I say don't give them a reason.'

'You told them he killed Lars.'

Mick laughed again.

'You don't get how it is around here,' he said. 'That's what they said and I agreed with them, that's all. If I agree with them, it keeps my daughter safe. If I don't agree with them, I'm putting her in the way of danger. In the end, they'll do what they want anyway.'

Eve picked up the plate of food.

'We ain't paying for this.'

Mick looked away from her.

'Take it. I've got customers waiting.'

At the lock-up, Wesley kept an eye out for the Viperines as Eve passed the plate of food through to Stranger. His words were muffled by the stone walls but his tone of voice said that he was grateful.

'Are we going back to eat at the saloon?' Wesley said.

'Do you feel like going back there? We got coffee and hard tack in the wagon.'

As they passed the entrance to the stable, Eve ducked

inside to pick-up Stranger's gun belt and the second pistol. She raked the straw aside where she had buried it, but it was gone. She tried in other places, thinking she had misremembered the spot but came up with nothing. Wesley helped her: still nothing. Remy and Charles had been back.

Wesley led the way to their wagon with his gun in his hand. At every corner he expected the Viperines to be waiting. Eve climbed into the wagon in search of their supplies while Wesley found enough kindling. He kept an eye out for intruders as he worked the flint and blew on the cotton wad in his hand.

They unloaded two chairs from the wagon and waited for the coffee.

'You ain't wearing your bonnet,' Wesley observed.

'It's right here.'

Eve pulled the cotton bonnet out of the pocket of her dress. She reached behind her head, scooped her long hair, wound it round her hand and fastened it into to a bun.

'It's a sun bonnet and there ain't no sun so I don't need it.'

She turned to Wesley.

'I got a scar on my face. I didn't put it there. People want to stare or look away, that's up to them.'

'Folks would say you were brave to do that.'

'Folks say a lot of things, some of them to your face, some of them when you're turned away.'

'You don't mind . . .' Wesley began.

'. . . mind them seeing?' Eve said. 'Why should I? It's telling the truth ain't it? This is who I am. Not someone

79

anonymous covered by a long dress and a bonnet that hides her face.'

Wesley chuckled good naturedly.

'Tellin' me you'll be wearing britches next?'

'When I wrote you that letter, I made up a name and I made up a story about myself because I was scared you'd take one look at my face and turn me away. But you didn't. You looked at me and you said come right along.'

Wesley considered her words.

'Paying me a compliment?'

'I am. But what if I told you I was married and I was running off? What would you have said then?'

Wesley smiled and shook his head slowly.

'Know what I'd say now.'

'Remember what Stranger said about how there wasn't no law out here, only people? About how some of 'em do right and some of 'em don't?'

'I remember,' Wesley said.

'Back East, there's a law says I've got to stay with Joe. Out here there's just right and wrong.'

The lid of the percolator started to rattle and the smell of coffee rose on the air. They both stared into the fire and watched the yellow flames curl.

'That's the reason we came out here, ain't it?' Wesley said. 'To live our own life in our own place without anybody telling us do this or do that. It's the simplest thing and most folks back East couldn't handle it.'

A sound made them look up. A footstep. Wesley reached for his gun and glanced at Eve. Her hand clutched the empty bonnet that had previously disguised

Stranger's gun. They froze and listened to the fire spit. There was another sound. Someone was inching towards them along the stable wall. Each step was light and carefully placed. Wesley raised his gun and took aim into the shadows at the corner as the steps got close. Eve held her breath.

Dainty stepped out of the shadows, balancing a plate of slapjacks in each hand. Holding the plates level, she walked slowly, kept her eyes fixed on them and occasionally glanced up to check her direction. Her pretty, oval face was wholly preoccupied with not spilling the food. Wesley smiled with relief and slipped the gun back into his holster. Eve took the plates.

'You've brought this over for us?'

Unsmiling, Dainty handed over the food.

'Come and eat with us,' Eve said kindly. 'Sit with us a while.'

'Pa says I got to get back because we're busy and I ain't to take no money from you.'

'You thank your pa,' Wesley said. 'And thank you, Dainty, for bringing this over to us.'

'Pa said he was expectin' you to come back to the saloon but you never came, so he told me to bring this over to you.'

'Your pa's lucky to have you to help him,' Eve said. 'I bet he don't know what he'd do without you.'

Dainty looked up at her. There were dark shadows under her eyes and where there should have been signs of laughter, the corners of her mouth were drawn down. She took two forks out of her pocket and handed them to Eve.

'Pa says I ain't to dally talkin',' Dainty said.

'Thank you, Dainty,' Wesley said. 'I mean that.'

Dainty stared at him for a moment and then turned and hurried into the shadows beside the stable.

Wesley took a plate from Eve and stabbed the pile of slapjacks with his fork. The taste of salt and the smell of pork fat reminded him of how hungry he was. Eve sat down beside him.

'Never thought Mick had it in him,' Wesley said through a mouthful of food.

'That little girl,' Eve said. 'She looks exhausted.'

They stared into the fire as they ate. Sounds from the square on the other side of the stable died away as night closed over the fort. There was the occasional stamp from one of the horses, the scuffle of a rat in the shadows and the crackle of dry sticks in the fire. Wesley put down his plate and poured two mugs of oily coffee.

Both of them failed to hear Remy approach until he stepped right into the ring of firelight. Wesley went for his gun but held off when he saw that Remy had Dainty by the hand. The little girl's expressionless face stared at them.

'Seems like I'm always bringing you information,' Remy began.

'Let her go.' Eve jumped to her feet. 'You got no right to hold her.'

Charles stepped into the pool of light. He nursed a twelve gauge, his finger was on the trigger and the barrel was an inch away from the back of Dainty's head. Remy laughed.

'Me and Dainty are friends, ain't we Dainty?'

Remy squeezed the little girl's hand. She looked up at him but her face was empty. He brought his other hand from behind his back. It held Stranger's gun belt. Both Starrs were in the holsters.

'Came back for that troublesome fella's belt and found there was a pistol missing.' Remy's voice was full of innocent surprise. 'Figured you must have given it back to him. That made me obliged to recover it. Then I met young Dainty here and she helped me, didn't you, Dainty? She stood right there whilst that man passed his gun out through the lock-up window.'

The little girl looked up at him.

'Pa says I ain't to dally talkin'.'

'You should do what your Pa says,' Remy said. He released her hand. 'You be a good girl and run along now.'

Dainty obediently hurried away into the shadows.

'That gun your friend had. Must have been intending to use it on me or my brothers when we let him out in the morning,' Remy laughed. 'You fools just made things a whole lot worse for yourselves.'

Charles covered Eve and Wesley with the shotgun as the two brothers stepped back out of the firelight and into the darkness.

8

The wagon train pulled into the fort in the middle of the morning. The heavy wagons were drawn by teams of oxen, the lighter ones by mules. Men and women trudged along beside them, trail dust clinging to their clothes and faces. They had only been walking since sunup, so they had the energy to talk and laugh together while the children hung back in groups playing games and exchanging secrets. Henry Winter was out in front. Joe's wagon came in last.

As the wagons formed a ring round the edge of the square, everyone from the post came out to stare at the new arrivals. The Tolsons and their customers stood at the door to the store; Mick, Dainty and a group of diners emerged from the saloon tent; men and women climbed down from the wagons which were already parked up; the two guys on the tops of their ladders who had been preparing the woodwork for a new sign over the store stopped work. Wesley and Eve stood beside the livery stable.

Henry Winter oversaw the drawing up of the wagons

and made sure each was as tight as it could be to the one in front. The drivers climbed down and called on their wives to help them lift the heavy yokes off the oxen and unhitch the mules from their harness. Winter walked the length of the train until he came to Joe's wagon.

'No need to park up so close,' Winter said. 'There's plenty of room.'

Joe scowled, turned away and worked on freeing his horses from their reins.

'You can't do this,' Joe said. 'A man can't cross this country alone.'

'What you were intending to do when we found you,' Winter said abruptly.

Joe gave his horse a vicious slap.

'Thought you were trying to save me.'

'We kept you away from the bottle while you were with us,' Winter said. 'That's something. When we learned what you'd done to your wife that was different.'

'I suppose you had a meeting,' Joe sneered.

'That's right and we decided that we didn't want you on the train no more.'

'What passed between me and my wife ain't none of your business.'

'You know why those good people on the train don't want you with them no more?'

Joe let go of the reins he was unfastening and turned to face Winter.

'You hypocrite.' Joe's eyes narrowed with contempt. 'You make out you're better than everybody else with your singin' and your your prayin'. You've decided to abandon a man in the middle of this godforsaken prairie.'

'I've already told you the reason you can't ride with our train no more is that you ain't showed no sign of repentance for the terrible thing you did.'

'That's your high and mighty ways talkin',' Joe laughed. 'I'd drunk some, I admit that. So I did it. I didn't wholly intend it, but I did. What you ain't askin' is why. Nothing happens without a reason.'

'Tell me then,' Winter said calmly. 'Why did you do it?'

'Obvious, ain't it?' Joe said. 'She drove me to it. She said she was going to leave me.'

Winter stepped away from him.

'I didn't intend it,' Joe went on. 'So how can it be my fault? How can you blame me? Anyway,' he added. 'She's my wife and I aim to take her with me. If she don't want to come, that's too bad.'

Having overheard the exchange between Joe and Henry Winter, Eve and Wesley stepped back into the shadows. Joe returned to unfastening the harness and Henry Winter walked away.

The guys up the ladders started to fasten a new sign which ran the length of the storefront. It read 'Viperine's Grocery and General', in high ox-blood capitals. Underneath, in smaller letters, were the words 'Manager J. Tolson Esq.'.

Wesley left Eve at her vantage point overlooking the square and went in search of the wagon which carried

86

their axle. Eve kept her eyes on Joe. She watched him finish with the harness, tie the horses to the side of the wagon and give them a cursory brush down. After that, he headed straight for the saloon tent. She knew he would be in there for the rest of the day. As Wesley and some of the men from the train returned with the axle, Eve slipped away to the store.

Ma Tolson proudly showed off the pile of cotton prints to a group of women while men from the wagons ordered supplies. The men took their tins of Bull Durham with them and went outside for a smoke. Eve waited for Ma to finish.

'I want some clothes,' Eve said.

'Well, dear, you had a good look at the prints the other day. Have you settled on one you like?'

'Work clothes,' Eve interrupted. 'And a hat.'

'You mean a bonnet, dear? Why, you could sew one yourself and save yourself a dollar—'

'Work clothes like men wear,' Eve insisted. 'And a hat.'

'Oh, I'm sorry, dear. I thought you meant the clothes were for you, not Wesley.'

'They are for me,' Eve said. 'I want britches, a jacket, boots and a hat.'

Ma Tolson stared her. 'You're so pretty, dear, if you'd just cover up that scar. Why do you want to wear men's clothes?'

'They're just clothes, Ma. They don't belong to men or women.'

Ma Tolson looked blank.

'But they're the clothes men wear, dear.'

'Can you help me?' Eve said.

'Pa usually deals with the men's clothes,' Ma Tolson said doubtfully.

Eve pointed to a shelf of work shirts and britches.

'They're up there. Can I use the steps and take a look?'

While Ma hovered at the foot of the stepladder, Eve pulled the clothes she needed out of the piles on the high shelf. She picked out a saddle jacket, a cotton shirt without a collar, work pants and a pair of the cheapest boots. Finally, to the amusement of the other customers she tried on a selection of hats usually bought by men in front of the store mirror. She settled on a grey plains-man because it was the best fit while Ma totalled the bill.

'What's going on, Eve?' Pa Tolson said.

'Cotton dress and a sun bonnet is fine for a New York coffee house,' Eve said. 'Ain't suited to a two thousand mile walk across the prairie.'

'All the other women do it,' Pa said.

'Yes, they do,' Eve said and left him to make up his own mind what she meant.

The rush of customers from the wagon train had died down by then and only Eve was left in the store.

'I want something else,' Eve said.

'Don't tell me it's a tin of tobacco,' Pa Tolson said. 'You got just about everything else a fella usually walks out of here with.'

'How much is your cheapest gun?'

'Now, Eve,' Pa Tolson said. 'Does Wesley know about this?'

'I'll tell him,' Eve said. 'Soon enough.'

Tolson saw how determined she was.

'We don't sell guns as a rule,' he said. 'I've got a couple out back I took in exchange for supplies. If you're set on it, you better come on through.'

Pa laid out two pistols on the store room table. One was an old Kentucky, a hand crafted, single-shot, muzzle loader. The cherry wood handle and barrel case were polished to a hard shine and brass fittings glinted in the light from the store window. The second was a compact Colt Patterson five-shot. Its milled steel chamber and barrel was clean and oiled and the beech wood handle was unadorned.

'How much?' Eve said.

'You'll want the Baby Patterson,' he said. 'It ain't accurate unless you're real close.'

She felt Pa Tolson's eye drift to the scar on her cheek.

'I can't sell these now. Everyone wants Navy Colts. The new six-shooters are more accurate and they got greater range. You say this is for your own protection?'

Eve felt his eyes on her scar again. She nodded.

'You take it then.' He pushed the Paterson across the table towards her. 'Let's hope you won't have to use it.'

'Thank you,' Eve said.

She liked the solid feel of the gun. With her hand closed on the grip, her thumb was in easy reach of the hammer. She held it up and squinted along the barrel then replaced it on the trestle.

'Heard about the meeting?' Pa Tolson said.

Eve picked up the Patterson again and weighed it in her hand.

'That fella they got locked up,' Pa continued. 'As we ain't got no courthouse nor no judge, Landry's gonna hold a meeting in here tonight. Viperines are gonna be judge and jury.'

'In the store?'

'Good a place as any.'

Eve stared at the gun in her hand.

'They got a witness who saw old Lars get shot,' Pa Tolson added. 'It'll be his word against the other fella's.'

'Why are they changing the sign?'

'Changing everything,' Tolson said. 'Viperines own the store so they can call it what they like. Since the troopers left there ain't no point in arguing.'

'Don't seem right,' Eve said.

Pa Tolson stared at the floor. 'Me and Ma are thinking about quitting. Set out for California when we were younger, then we got kinda sidetracked into running the store and the years just slipped by. This is as far as we got along the trail. Ain't been easy but it's been a steady kind of life. Anyhow,' he smiled faintly, 'you best hurry along, before Ma sees me giving you the gun.'

'You got anywhere I could change?' Eve said. 'I want to get used to these work clothes.'

'Right here,' Tolson said. 'I'll leave you alone. Got a back entrance if you want to use it.'

A short while later, Eve emerged from the store with the Patterson bundled in her cotton dress. The work clothes were stiff and new. But she liked the feel of the boots. Even though they were the smallest size and she had to stuff them with paper, they gave her a sense of power each time her heel bit the ground. As she strode across the square no one gave her a second glance.

Behind the livery stable, Wesley and the men worked at fitting the axle. Wesley did a double take.

The wagon was unloaded and their possessions were stacked neatly in the yard. Wesley and another man held up the empty wagon while two more struggled with the axle. Eve took Wesley's place to allow him to score guidelines on the wood where the fit was too tight. Then they lowered the wagon and laid the axle flat to plane it down.

'Something I need to do,' Eve said.

While the men concentrated on their woodwork, Eve tucked the pistol into her belt and strolled out into the square. The men were now putting up a name board over Lars' workshop which read 'Viperine's Carpentry' painted in the same ox-blood capitals.

Eve headed for the saloon tent to find Mick. Joe was sitting alone at a far table staring into space in some rotgut-fueled reverie and failed to notice her. A newspaper was spread in front of him. Mick recognized her straight off and stared at her.

'Taking any food over to the lock-up today?' Eve said.

'What are you dressed like that for?'

'Practical,' Eve said. 'For what I got to do.'

'Charles said he'd be round about midday,' Mick said. 'To take a plate over to the prisoner.'

'Do something for me?' Eve said. 'Don't let Dainty go with him this time.'

Mick scowled at her.

At the sound of her name, Dainty appeared in her

grubby pinafore at the kitchen entrance. Her solemn face broke into a grin when she saw Eve's outfit. Eve knelt down, took off her hat and dropped it on Dainty. Far too big, it fell down to her nose. The little girl giggled and pushed it back so she could see.

'Look at me, Pa.'

'Heard there's gonna be a meeting,' Eve said.

Mick's face hardened.

'What if there is?'

'You gonna speak against Stranger?'

Mick looked down at Dainty.

'Give the lady her hat back now. You got your chores.'

'I want one, Pa.' Dainty gave a twirl and the hat slid round her head. 'Can I have a hat like this one, Pa?'

Her smile vanished when she saw her father's hangdog expression and she handed the hat to Eve.

'I'll buy you a hat,' Eve whispered. 'If your pa don't mind.'

Mick shrugged. Dainty peeped at Eve from round the flap of the tent before she disappeared back to the kitchen.

Outside the tent, the sun was high and the day was bright. The heavy atmosphere which had oppressed the plains over the past few days had blown away and in the air the scent of sage was fresh and new. Eve took a seat furthest from the entrance. A group of men from the wagon train sat at a nearby trestle rolling cigarettes. When they eventually recognized her, they smiled at her clothes which were pretty much identical to their own. She watched the guys climb down their ladders after fixing the sign over the carpentry shop and stand chatting while they decided what to move on to next. More new sign boards lay at their feet.

People came and went between the wagons and the store. Every now and then, Eve could hear Mick's irritable voice raised at one or other of the cooks back behind the saloon tent. There was no sign of Wesley or Henry Winter, so Eve presumed the axle must be giving them more trouble than they had thought. Eventually, she noticed Charles heading across the square towards her. But he too hadn't noticed her and marched straight through the entrance of the tent. A few minutes later he emerged holding slapjacks and a bottle of water. Eve caught the scent of hot fat as he passed her. She let him reach the edge of the square and then got to her feet, pulled her hat down low and followed him.

When Charles was opposite the livery, there was a holler and he turned. Eve snatched at the brim of her hat and covered her face. Remy waved from outside the store and pointed gleefully up at the new sign. Charles shouted a reply and turned back in the direction of the lock-up. For a moment, Eve thought Remy was going to cross the square but then he headed into the store.

Charles put the plate and bottle down outside the iron door of the lock-up while he delved in his pocket for the key. He looked up at the sound of Eve's footsteps but her face was hidden by the brim of her new plainsman. Not recognizing her, he looked away and banged on the door.

There was a muffled answer from inside.

'Brought you some chow. When I unlock this door the plate'll be in front of you and I'll be here with my Navy Colt trained at your head, so don't you try nothin'. You just pick-up the plate and step back inside.'

Eve waited for Charles to unlock the door. He turned the heavy iron key with one hand, slid his gun out of its holster with the other and backed away from the door. As the door swung open, Eve jumped forward and gouged Charles in the small of his back with the barrel of the five-shot.

'Drop it,' she yelled.

Shock lost Charles a moment of his life. Then Stranger sprang at him from the open doorway, grabbed him round the legs and tipped him backwards cracking the back of his skull on the hard ground. Eve leapt out of the way, keeping her aim steady. Charles's pistol flew out of his hand. Stranger disentangled himself from his legs, flung back his arm and before Charles realized what was happening, landed an anvil punch on his jaw.

Eve grabbed one of Charles's legs while Stranger took the other. Together they hauled him into the lock-up, threw the food and water in after him and heaved the iron door shut. Stranger turned the key.

It was only then that Eve saw Stranger's swollen face. A boot-heel gash caked in dried blood split the florid bruise which covered his right cheek. Above it, his eye was narrowed to a slit.

'I got to get out of sight,' he said.

9

Swaying slightly, Joe stood outside the door marked 'Officers', clenched his fist and rapped. He stepped a pace back and waited until Remy cautiously opened the door a couple of inches. He checked each way to be sure no one else was there and stared contemptuously at Joe. An ingratiating smile slid across Joe's mouth.

'Can I come in?'

'Why?' Remy glared at him.

'Got something to discuss.'

'What?'

Scowling, Landry pushed his brother aside and opened the door wide. He nodded to Joe to come in.

The room was empty except for pairs of bunk beds along opposite walls, an iron stove, a table and three hard chairs. Blankets were strewn over three of the bunks, the stove was unlit and a pack of greasy playing cards sat in the middle of the table. Stranger's gun belt with its pistols in the holsters hung over the back of one of the chairs.

Landry gestured Joe to sit while he and Remy leaned

against the table in front of him.

'Come to offer my services,' Joe said.

'You've been drinkin'',' Landry snapped.

He waved away the liquor fumes.

'Those hymn singers have thrown me off the train,' Joe explained quickly. 'Got to wait for more wagons to come through before I can move on.'

Landry and Remy glared down at him.

'Thought maybe I could work for you guys.'

'Doin' what?' Landry said.

'Kinda like the way you got things going round here,' Joe blustered. 'Thought I could help you out. I'm quick with a gun. Somebody needs tellin' what to do I can tell 'em.'

Laughter rattled in Landry's throat.

'You're the guy that cut his wife ain't you?' he said. 'What kind of a man does that?'

'Wasn't meant to happen,' Joe said quietly.

'Round here we pick fights with men and like the women lookin' pretty.'

Landry stared down at Joe.

'Seen some lowlifes in my time but never met anyone who would do something like that.'

'I could be useful to you,' Joe protested.

'You stink of rotgut,' Landry said. 'Only place you could be useful is the saloon.'

Pa Tolson arranged the newspapers on the trestle at the front of the store with as much attention as if he were laying a starched tablecloth in a Boston restaurant. Henry Winter had brought in a bag containing the mail, newspapers and the usual array of wanted posters. As soon as word got round, the store would be full. He and Ma braced themselves. He shuffled through the pile of mail. Most of it was for people who had passed through weeks ago. Tolson would return these letters to Henry Winter who would produce them again at successive forts along the trail until he caught up the people to whom they were addressed or he handed them in at the post office in San Francisco.

The Wanted posters were curiosities out here: Tolson never bothered to display them. There were details of robberies, murders and rewards, sometimes illustrated by line drawings of young men's shocked faces. They provided a glimpse into the underside of life hundreds of miles away and were of no relevance. But the newspapers were different.

No one cared if the news was three or four months old. Out here, isolated by a thousand miles of empty prairie, reading the news was like looking through the wrong end of a telescope: everything seemed so far away that when events had taken place hardly mattered. Readers scanned the pages for the mention of the names they recognized, famous people they had heard of or places they knew.

News stories fed the readers' opinions about goings-on in Washington and encouraged them to comment on what the president should do. They forgot that these events were already long past and that the government's pronouncements had already been heard. The debates the newspapers engendered in the fort made it a kind of parallel world in which people argued about the outcome of events which had already happened.

Henry Winter had done a good job. He had brought an array of titles and kept them bundled in oil cloth so they arrived in good condition. Recently, all the wagon trains brought were copies of the *The Oregon Spectator*, read by so many people that they were falling apart. But this time there was the *New York Tribune*, *The National Era* and a pile of *The Friends Review*. With war coming, each news article was a lightning bolt: Oregon had entered the US as a free state; the debate was burning between free staters and pro slavers in Kansas; Captain Brown had led an attack on an armory at Harpers Ferry, Virginia and was now on trial for treason.

Pa Tolson stood in the doorway of the store ready to tell passers-by about the newly arrived news but it was the afternoon lull and no one was about. One of the men from the wagon train, staggering slightly, crossed the square. Two of Landry's men were erecting a post on each side of the entrance to the saloon tent. Beside them on the ground lay another sign in ox-blood capitals.

Until now, Tolson had never bothered about the Viperines' land claims. He paid his rent like all the other traders and life went on. War coming in the East had shaken everybody up and with the troopers gone, things looked different. Maybe it really was time for him and Ma to load up a wagon and claim an acreage in California. The Viperines didn't just want to own the fort; they wanted to control everyone in it.

Landry leaned forward in his chair, riffled the pack of

cards and dealt a poker hand, alternating cards from the top then the bottom of the pack.

'See me do that?'

Remy sat opposite him.

'What?'

Landry gave a hoarse laugh, swept up the cards and dealt again. He looked at Remy expectantly.

'What?' Remy said.

'I'm lookin' forward to the next hand of poker with you,' Landry said.

Remy scowled. 'Dunno what you're talking about.'

'Charles took food to the lock-up hours ago,' Landry said. 'Where do you reckon he is?'

Remy shrugged. 'How should I know?'

Landry snapped the cards together, pushed his chair back from the table and stood up. Remy jumped to his feet.

'Going to look for him?'

His grabbed Stranger's gun belt and the double action Starrs, unbuckled his own belt and slid Stranger's round his hips.

'Had my eye on these,' Remy said.

He drew one of the pistols and examined the twin triggers. The forward trigger fired the gun and the rear trigger cocked the hammer and rotated the chamber. A practiced hand could shoot and recock in a single motion and double the rate of fire. Remy whistled admiringly through his teeth.

'Ain't seen nothing like this before.'

Landry led the way to the saloon tent. A new sign in

dark red capitals hung over the door: 'Saloon Viperine' and underneath in smaller letters 'whiskey, beer and chow. Manager M. Duggan'. Inside, a few late afternoon drinkers sat at the trestles. Joe studied a newspaper in a corner with a half empty bottle in front of him. Mick looked up when he saw Landry enter and wiped his hands on his apron.

'Charles? Ain't seen him since he collected the food,' Mick said briefly in answer to Landry's question. Sweat stood out on his putty face.

'Saw him head for the lock-up?' Landry snapped.

'Saw him leave holding a plate of slapjacks which he ain't paid for,' Mick said.

As Landry turned to go, Mick said 'You still holding this meeting?'

'Nine o'clock in the store. I want everyone to be there to see justice done.'

Mick's eye fell on Remy's new gun belt and he bit back his words.

Landry hammered on the iron door to the lock-up. Someone groaned from inside.

'Who's in there?' he shouted.

'It's him, ain't it?' Remy said excitedly. He drew one of the Starrs from its holster and scanned the square.

'They jumped me.' Charles's muffled voice came from inside the lock-up.

'You can't do nothing right,' Landry snapped. Then he noticed Remy waving Stranger's gun. 'Put that thing away.'

Remy holstered the gun.

'See who jumped you?'

'Short fella,' came Charles's voice. 'Didn't recognize him.'

'I know who it was,' Remy said. 'That fella who's got the wagon with the busted axle. Must have been him.'

'Stocky guy with a round face,' Remy shouted through the door.

'He was real small,' Charles shouted back. 'Carried a five-shot. I never got a proper look at him.'

'A five-shot?' Landry said. 'Who uses a five-shot nowadays?'

'You gonna let me out?' Charles yelled.

'Would do if we had a key.' Remy laughed.

'That fella with the busted axle,' Landry said. 'Better go find him.'

As daylight started to fade, the smell of wood smoke from the saloon fires hung in the air. Black clouds massed over the prairie to the east and the blood-red sunset reflected in the windows of the store. Groups of people from the wagons sauntered in the direction of food. A breeze got up out of nowhere, shook the canvas of the saloon tent, snatched dust from the ground and threw it into the eyes of the people crossing the square. Blinded for a moment, they ducked their heads away from the wind and kneaded their eyes with the backs of their hands. As quickly as the breeze had come, it died like a warning they barely had time to heed.

Wesley and the others finished fitting the new axle and stood back to admire their work. Eve, now wearing her cotton dress again, waited for the coffee to boil on the fire. They looked up sharply when Landry and Remy stepped out from round the stable into the yard.

'Wanted to make sure you're all comin' to the meeting,' Landry said. 'In the store. Nine o'clock. Concerns everyone who's in the fort right now.'

Henry Winter and his men stared at him, stony-faced. Eve stared at the gun belt Remy was wearing.

Landry turned to Wesley. 'One more thing,' he said. 'What kind of sidearm do you carry, mister?'

Wesley raised his arms.

'Ain't packin' right now.'

'I can see that,' Landry said coldly. 'Fetch your weapon for me, will you?'

'What's this about?' Wesley said. 'I ain't fetching nothing.'

Landry drew his Colt and nodded to Remy.

'You won't mind if we take a look in your wagon,' Landry said.

Remy held one of Stranger's pistols in his hand.

'We're looking for a guy that carries a five-shot.'

'No one uses a five-shot no more,' Wesley said. 'You're crazy.'

'We're also lookin' for that friend of yours who busted out of the lock-up. Seems like a guy with a five-shot helped him.'

Wesley crossed over to the wagon, reached behind the tailboard and pulled out his gun belt. A Navy Colt hung in the holster.

'Satisfied?'

Landry holstered his gun and turned to Henry Winter.

'What about you others?'

'We don't carry guns. Got a Sharps for hunting, that's all.'

Eve stood up and faced Remy.

'That ain't your gun belt you're wearing, mister. Those ain't your guns neither.'

Remy laughed and stuck the pistol back in its holster.

'Them's Starr double-actions,' Eve continued. 'There's only one man around here carries them and he's a friend of mine. I want you to unbuckle your belt right now and hand them to me.'

Incredulous, Remy stared at her for a second, then he turned to Landry.

'Hear this? She's talking about Starr double-actions.'

Eve raised her hand and thrust her sun bonnet close to Remy's chest as if she was asking him to take it from her. He rounded on her.

'What's this?' he spluttered.

He snatched the cotton bonnet out of Eve's hand and threw it down into the dirt. It was only then he saw that the bonnet had disguised a pistol, which was now levelled at his face. He staggered a pace backwards.

Landry went for his gun, but his hand froze over the holster as he heard the snick of Wesley's Colt being cocked.

'Ain't saying it again,' Eve said.

Remy stared at her, barely able to comprehend what was going on.

Wesley waved his Colt at Landry.

'Drop it right now.'

Landry plucked his gun from its holster and let it fall

in front of him. Wesley kicked it aside.

'Do what she says,' Landry hissed.

Remy seemed to snap into focus. Anger blazed in his face.

'You do what you like, brother. I ain't having my gun took off me by a—'

Eve lowered her aim and shot him in the arm.

Remy howled.

'All right, all right. Have the guns. I don't want 'em.'

Sobbing with pain and rage, he struggled with the buckle and let the gun belt fall.

Wesley snatched up Landry's pistol, flicked open the chamber and let the shells spill into the dirt. He handed the gun back to him and looked him in the eye.

'Eve was reclaiming property that rightfully belonged to someone else,' Wesley said. 'That's all. There was a misunderstanding about whether it was going to be returned. Count it as an accident if you like. We can keep this between us.'

Remy gasped and gripped his arm as blood welled between his fingers. Landry's face was stone.

'That's a five-shot,' he said.

Eve faced him. 'Yes it is.'

10

Landry strode across the square in the dying light. Still clutching his wounded arm, Remy staggered after him.

'You won't say nothing about who shot me, will you?'

Landry ignored his brother's plea and quickened his pace. Remy whimpered with pain as each footstep jolted his arm.

'I think the bullet's still in there. Burns like fire.'

'Shut up,' Landry hissed. 'I got one brother in the lock-up and the other shot by a woman. Am I supposed to do everything on my own?'

Landry flung aside the canvass door to the saloon tent, eyeballed Joe sitting at a corner trestle with the *New York News* spread out in front of him and marched straight over. Remy slumped into a chair, still clutching his arm.

'You said you wanted to work for me,' Landry snapped.

Joe looked up at Landry and then at Remy, whose face was tight with pain.

'Something change your mind?' Joe said. An insolent smile flickered across his mouth.

'Someone busted Stranger out of the lock-up,' Landry said. 'Small-built guy. Uses a five-shot.'

'Patterson five-shot? Didn't know anyone still carried them.'

'Someone going to take a look at this arm?' Remy said. 'I can feel the bullet. Sure of it.'

'I want you to find this Stranger and the guy who busted him out and bring them to me,' Landry continued. 'Shoot 'em if you have to.'

'Where am I supposed to find 'em?' Joe said.

'That wife of yours is carrying the five-shot. She'll know where they are.'

Remy began to slip his arm out of his shirt. His face was screwed up and he gasped for breath.

'Constance?' Joe said. 'She caused all this?'

'Cleaning my gun,' Remy said. 'Didn't know there was a slug left in the chamber.'

Joe laughed. He looked at Landry.

'Understand why you need some help. What's in it for me?'

'Fifty dollars,' Landry said.

'Each,' Joe snapped.

'Fifty dollars each alive,' Landry said. 'Wound 'em if you have to. I got to present them at this meeting tonight. Show people what we're dealing with. Prove to 'em why we need the Militia Charge.'

Remy gingerly peeled the shirt off his arm.

'I can't look at it,' Remy gasped. 'Slug's still in there. I can feel it.'

Landry grabbed his arm and peered at the wound. He splashed Joe's whiskey over it and let his arm drop.

'Flesh wound,' Landry said. 'Ain't no slug in there. Barely a scratch and I reckon that's what she meant to do. Pretty nice shooting if it was.'

'She?' Joe said.

'Button it,' Remy said. 'I still got my shooting arm.'

'You got two hours,' Landry said to Joe. 'Called the meeting for nine.'

'Gonna help me?' Joe smirked at Remy. 'With your shooting arm?'

Remy shook his head.

'Got to get my brother out of the lock-up,' Remy said. 'I'll have to bust out the bars to do it.'

Joe folded the newspaper and stood up. He drew his colt, checked the chamber and reholstered his gun.

'Start looking behind the livery stable,' Landry said.

Pa Tolson had just lit the oil lamps in the store when Eve pushed open the door. The pile of cotton prints had been moved back against the wall and the sacks of dry goods were piled in front of the counter. In their place, rows of benches had been set out in front of a table and chair which faced the door.

'You're early,' Tolson said. 'Meeting don't start till nine.'

'Come for another sack of flour,' Eve said. 'Gave ours to some folks who did us a good turn.'

Pa Tolson heaved a sack on to the counter.

'What happened to your work clothes?' he said lightly.

'Ain't working right now,' Eve said. 'Got any candy?'

'Sweet tooth?' He grinned. 'Me too.'

107

'For Dainty. We'll be heading out at first light. Wanted to give her something before we go.'

Tolson lifted a tall jar down from a shelf behind the counter.

'Ma makes these boiled sugars. They're Dainty's favourites.'

'I'll take them,' Eve said.

'The whole jar?'

'Sure,' Eve said. 'That kid deserves more than boiled sugars. And have you got a hat small enough to fit Dainty?'

'She never had anyone buy her presents before,' Tolson laughed. 'She won't know what to think. You already bought my smallest hat this afternoon. If I were you, I'd fold a ring of newspaper inside it and let her wear yours.'

Eve fished in her purse for the right coins, picked up the flour sack under one arm and the candy jar under the other, thanked him and headed for the door.

'Ma's gonna be real pleased Dainty is going to have her candy,' Tolson called after her.

On her way back across the square, Eve heard shouting from the direction of the lock-up. Remy was supervising busting Charles out. One of his sleeves was rolled up and there was a cotton bandage tied round his arm. An ox from the wagon train had been roped to the window bars and a crowd had gathered to watch as the animal hauled the iron grid away in an explosion of dust and falling masonry. There was a terrified shout from inside, then Charles crawled through the hole and tumbled to the ground. He picked himself up and

108

slapped the mortar dust off his clothes. Eve smiled and headed for the saloon.

Earlier, with Eve gone to the store, Stranger climbed out of the wagon and sat on the tailboard. Wesley built up the fire and pushed the coffee pot closer to the flames.

'Welcome to ride along with us,' Wesley said. 'We leave at first light. Aim to put as many miles as I can between this place and us by tomorrow night.'

'Start at dawn,' Stranger said. 'And never say goodbye. Best way to begin a journey. Concerned the Viperines will come after you?'

'Wanting their Militia Charge?' Wesley said. 'If we ain't got no choice, then we'll pay. Don't make it right though.'

'No, it don't,' Stranger said. 'But Remy's carryin' a grudge now. He'll be wantin' to shoot somebody and I reckon he ain't concerned whether it's you, me or Eve.'

'Like I said,' Wesley said. 'You can come along with us. Got more of a chance if there's three of us.'

Stranger shook his head. 'Travelling east,' he said. 'Missouri.'

'Everyone else on the trail is heading west,' Wesley said.

Stranger picked his feet up and moved back into the wagon to lean against one of the packing cases. He was out of sight of the yard. His voice fell almost to a whisper as though he reflected on his words as he spoke.

'Been on the frontier most of my life. Been a scout,

109

a guide, a hunter, even a lawman for a spell. Been back and forth on the Oregon Trail, in the mountains and on the prairies. Been as far west as a man can go, right to the blue ocean. Rode all over the land in the west folks call "the promised land". I've seen it all.'

'That's where we're headed,' Wesley said. 'Reckon we got the chance of a good life.'

'People there are just like people anywhere,' Stranger said. 'Mostly you meet them one day and the next they've moved on. Just got to try and do right by 'em. But there's a few who leave you with something. You carry a piece of them inside you wherever you go. They're the ones you owe; they're the ones you got to stay with. That's the lesson the trail teaches you and stands in judgement over you if you don't learn it.'

Wesley heard the lonesomeness behind Stranger's words and stared into the fire. The flames danced and the kindling crackled and spat.

'Ever killed anyone?'

Stranger hesitated.

'Comes with living my kind of life. Every time I draw my gun somebody dies.'

'That why you're heading for Missouri?'

'Got a brother lives there. Nice fella. Got a good spread of land and he tends it well. Carry a piece of him in me, his wife too. Just didn't realize it when I was younger.'

Stranger paused as if he was listening to his story, not telling it, and he was waiting for the words to come.

'We fell out like young fellas do.'

Wesley handed him a cup of coffee.

110

'He took a shine to the girl I was courting,' Stranger said. 'When it came down to it she had to choose. Him or me. She chose him and they married right off. Bought a place and they're still there.'

Stranger took a slug of coffee.

'Hated him at the time,' he continued. 'Hated both of them. Or thought I did. Told 'em they'd never see me again and lit out for the territories.'

Stranger stared into his coffee cup.

'She said I wasn't the marryin' kind. I didn't know what she was talking about but she was right. Even then I was considering leaving her at home and going off scouting for the army, though I hadn't told her. If the settled life had attracted me, that's the path I would have taken.'

Stranger took a last swig of coffee.

'Just want to go back and let them know I don't bear no grudges.'

A sound made Wesley look up, a footstep maybe. A second later, Joe rounded the corner of the stable, his Colt in his hand. He covered Wesley while he scanned the yard.

'Fresh out of coffee,' Wesley said.

'Were you talkin' to somebody?' Joe said.

Wesley looked around the yard.

'See anybody here?'

'Anybody in that wagon?'

Wesley stood up.

'No there ain't. What's your business here anyway?'

'Lookin' for a fella that carries one of them old five-shot pistols.'

111

'A Patterson?' Wesley said. 'No one uses them any more.'

'Someone does,' Joe said. 'A small-built fella. My wife knows who it is because he gave it to her.'

'What?'

'You know what I'm talking about,' Joe snarled. 'Where is she any way?'

'She ain't here.'

'Anyhow, I heard she shot a guy with it,' Joe sniggered. 'Winged him. Is that true?'

'Wouldn't know anything about that,' Wesley said.

'Mister,' Joe said coldly. 'We ain't getting very far. I'm working for the Viperines now and they're paying me to find two people for them. The other guy I'm looking for is that fella you rode in with. The one who busted out of the lock-up.'

Wesley shrugged.

'You can see there's no one here except me.'

'You gonna let me take a look in that wagon?'

Joe stepped forward. Then he looked hard at Wesley.

'Do I know you?'

Wesley stared at him.

'Have we met some place ?' Joe said.

'I'd remember,' Wesley said.

'Never realized it before,' Joe said. 'You look mighty familiar all of a sudden.'

'You been in the saloon?' Wesley said. 'First you're looking for a guy who carries a gun no one's used for years then you think you know me.'

A shadow of confusion crossed Joe's face.

'To hell with it. Are you gonna let me look in the

wagon?'

A cool breeze entered the yard, swept through the dust and made the fire dance. Wesley took a pace back.

'Mister, I can tell you I ain't about to allow nobody who works for the Viperines to go near my wagon.'

'You're crazy,' Joe said. 'I'm holding a gun.'

Eve came into the yard walking awkwardly under the weight of a sack of flour. She ignored Joe, pushed past the two men and heaved the sack over the tailboard of the wagon.

'I want to talk to you,' Joe said.

'I don't care what you want.'

'Where's the fella gave you that five-shot?'

'What are you talking about?'

'The fella who busted that guy out of the lock-up. I got orders to find 'em both.'

'Are you talking about the Patterson I shot Remy Viperine with?' Eve said.

'It was you,' Joe roared, delighted. 'I knew it. He tried to tell me it was an accident.'

'You mean this Patterson?'

Eve slipped the five-shot out of the pocket of her dress, thumbed back the hammer and pointed it straight at Joe.

'Woah,' Joe raised his hands. He still held his pistol. 'No need for that.'

'No need?' Eve said. 'After what you did to me? I should have shot you years ago.'

Joe was backing away now, past the fire towards the path at the side of the stable.

'Just tell me where the guy is who gave you the gun,'

Joe said. 'It's him I'm after.'

'You'll never catch him,' Eve said. 'He's too quick. Comes and goes before you know it.'

'What about the other fella, the one you rode in with?'

'What about him?'

Still walking backwards with his gun in the air and his eyes fixed on Eve's five-shot, Joe stumbled and nearly fell.

'Where is he?'

'Hiding.'

'Where?'

'If I knew, I wouldn't tell you, Joe. But he ain't here.'

'All right, all right.'

'Now I'm through talking to you, Joe,' Eve said patiently. 'I already shot one man today but I'd much rather shoot you. You know I mean that.'

Joe had reached the livery stable wall. Holding the five-shot steady and level with his chest, Eve stepped towards him. Joe peeled himself off the wall, ducked round the corner and hightailed it down the path to the square.

11

Joe found Remy and Charles patrolling the square. There was white dust in the weave of Charles' jacket, on his hat and in his beard; a rusty bloodstain showed through the bandage on Remy's arm.

'Landry says we gotta make sure everybody comes to the meeting.'

'Can't find 'em,' Joe said. 'You gotta help me.'

The last of the day's sunlight bled into the sky in the east, the temperature fell and the air was still. Smoke from the saloon fires hung over the fort and caught in the throats of people from the wagon train. Pa Tolson had lit torches and stood them in iron stands on either side of the door to the grocery.

'You're getting paid fifty bucks a head to find them,' Remy said. 'Why should we help you?'

'You know the place better than I do,' Joe protested. 'You know where they could be hiding.'

'Mostly when I want to find someone, I just keep walking round and sooner or later I bump into 'em,' Remy said. 'There ain't no hiding places.'

'When Landry's finished with that little fella, I want him,' Charles said.

'You mean the fella that jumped you and locked you up?' Remy sniggered. 'The one that covered you with an old five-shot.'

'You ain't no better,' Charles blustered. 'Just remember who shot you.'

Joe exploded with laughter. 'My wife. And she's practically young enough to be a girl. Didn't let her get away with nothing when she was with me.' His mouth was full of contempt. 'You thought you had a bullet in your arm and it wasn't nothin' but a scratch.'

'Coulda happened to anybody,' Remy snapped.

'Didn't, though,' Joe jeered. 'Happened to you.'

'You better find those people, mister,' Remy said. 'Else Landry is gonna be mad and you're gonna suffer.'

'Wait a minute,' Charles said. 'We got to try something else. Me and Remy'll go round the fort while you wait by the store. We'll round 'em up like cattle.'

'You reckon they'll come to the meeting?' Joe said.

'Have to. They'll be in the crowd, else we'll find 'em,' Charles explained. 'There ain't nowhere to hide in this fort. They're just giving you the runaround.'

'Sounds like an idea,' Joe said.

'Better than anything you've come up with,' Remy said. 'Did you look behind the livery like I said?'

' 'Course.'

Joe felt colour rise to his face but Remy didn't notice.

Dainty's face was a picture. She had her arm round the huge glass jar of boiled sugars, which stood beside her

116

on the trestle, and on her head was Eve's hat, stuffed with newspaper. Luxuriating in the little girl's rapturous smile, Eve sat opposite. From behind the bar, in between serving customers, Mick watched them closely.

'I'm gonna wear it to the meeting,' Dainty said. 'Pa says we got to close the saloon because everyone's got to go.'

'That ain't long now,' Eve said. 'Half an hour I guess.'

Across the saloon, Mick wiped his hands on his filthy apron and beckoned Wesley over. His putty face was anxious as usual.

'Something I want to ask you,' Mick began cautiously. 'I'll come straight out with it.'

Wesley rested his hands on the trestle.

'You got space in your wagon for two more? Me and the little one?'

'Quittin' the saloon?'

'Ain't no place for Dainty to grow up. Always knew we'd move on some day. Now it seems like the right time. With the troopers gone, Viperines can do what they like.'

'I saw the sign outside,' Wesley said.

'That ain't half of it. They just increased their charges by fifty per cent. If I don't get out now, I'll be paying them back rent from here till doomsday.'

'Eve'll think springtime has come early when she hears Dainty's coming along,' Wesley said. ' 'Course, you'll have to walk, mostly. Only one at a time can ride in the wagon.'

'I got some money saved and I can bring supplies,' Mick said.

'Told Landry about this?'

'Not yet.' Mick's face darkened. 'Shouldn't make no difference to him. The cooks will run the saloon. He knows they're good workers.'

'Careful how you tell him,' Wesley warned. 'Landry's the kind of guy who likes to make the decisions.'

'We ain't got much to bring so we won't take up much space in the wagon,' Mick said. 'Just a few clothes and blankets along with the supplies.'

'Toys for Dainty?'

Mick shook his head.

'Started to carve a doll for her once out of a piece of cottonwood. Never finished it. Since my wife passed, I've always been working and Dainty's been with me in the saloon.'

'Reckon you should tell Landry now,' Wesley said. 'No saying what kind of mood he'll be in after the meeting.'

Remy and Charles appeared at the entrance to the saloon.

'Now listen up,' Remy shouted. Conversation fell to a hush and Mick ducked through the opening to the kitchen to quieten the cooks. 'Meeting's in fifteen minutes over at the store,' Remy continued. 'All of you got to come. Landry's orders. Me and my brother will be making a sweep of all wagons and buildings at the start of the meeting. We don't want to find no one, understand?'

There was a mumble of agreement from across the

saloon as the diners went back to their food and the hum of conversation rose again.

Remy noticed Eve and pushed between the trestles to reach her. He stood opposite her, put the palms of his hands flat on the trestle and leaned over her until his face was almost touching hers.

'Still looking for a couple of fellas,' he said quietly.

Eve put her arm round Dainty.

'The little guy who put my brother in the lock-up and that fella who rode in with you. When we do the sweep, we're going to find 'em. Know what we're gonna do then?'

Eve pulled Dainty close. She was suddenly aware of the Patterson weighing down the pocket of her dress.

'Clear off right now,' Eve said coldly, 'or I'm going to stand up and tell this whole saloon how you come by that bandage on your arm.'

Remy pulled himself up to his full height and sneered down at her.

'Think anyone would believe you?'

'I would,' Dainty said firmly.

Remy coloured, reached down and chucked her under the chin.

'Cute, ain't she?'

He turned, barged through the saloon crowd again and rejoined Charles at the entrance.

'One more thing,' Remy called. 'Your husband's working with us now. Reckon after we find those other two, he'll be coming to pay you a visit. He ain't the kind of guy to let his wife run out on him.'

Remy and Charles slipped out of the saloon tent and

119

let the canvas flap fall after them. Eve looked across for Wesley and saw that he had been watching them with his hand on the handle of his gun. From the kitchen entrance, Mick called out that there would be no more service till after the meeting.

Outside in the flickering torchlight, Joe watched people from the wagons cross the square and head in the direction of the store. He stared at each of their faces but Stranger wasn't among them. Almost all the men from the wagons were tall and thin with weathered, angular faces. There wasn't a short man among them. Then there was Mick from the saloon who was built like a tub of lard and Pa Tolson who was tall. And this little guy was a puzzle. The hands who worked for the Viperines were all tough men used to physical work and hard drinking and had the square shoulders and round bellies to prove it. The smallest people in the fort were Mick's Chinese cooks. No way it could have been one of them. Joe would have to wait until Remy and Charles did the sweep. That would drive them out.

Landry was already inside sitting in the chair facing the door so he could look into the face of each person as they entered. Each of them caught his eye as they came in then looked away quickly. He knew they were afraid of him. So they should be.

The Viperine family had founded a trading post here when he and his brothers were boys. His mother and father had built the sod houses out by the main gate with their own hands. They had endured furnace heat in the summer and snow in the winter; his father had hunted buffalo and traded with the Sioux and when the first wagons came, he traded with them. He found himself on what people began to call the Oregon Trail and suddenly there was an opportunity for his sons which he had never dreamed of. The wagons kept coming. Their owners wanted guides, workshops for repairs, supplies and protection. But the pioneers' callous disrespect for the first nation who inhabited this land led to disturbance and conflict. The government in Washington, whose policy of settling the West was part of their bid to annex the whole continent, sent in the army. The army took over the Viperine family trading post and built a fort.

Sitting there on that evening, watching the people from the wagon train file into the store, Landry knew his time had come. Fort Dove was the Viperines' birthright and with the troopers gone, he was about to reclaim it. He already owned a store, a stable and a saloon. By imposing a Militia Charge on the wagons which passed through, he would soon be able to raise the capital to build a town. And he would own it all. The question he had been deliberating was how could he convince the pioneers to pay?

Landry came up with two ways. The first was that he and his brothers could go out and ambush a Sioux hunting party which would provoke an attack on the next wagon train which passed through. When word got round, the train after that would readily pay for Militia protection. But the Sioux were unpredictable. They might attack the fort and if they did, apart from incurring the obvious dangers, that would bring the troopers back, war or no war.

The second and safer way was to show the wagon trains that there was danger from within. He would show them what murderers and thieves there were in the West and how he had organized the capture of a murderer right here at Fort Dove. He would produce a reliable witness and if there was a witness there would be no need of a trial. The drifter who was to be accused had simply ended up in the wrong place at the wrong time and by the look of him he was used to that.

The door opened again and Mick Duggan barged through the crowd. As usual, his pasty face was frowning and he looked as if he had something on his mind. He stood in front of Landry and twisted his apron in his hands.

'Something I got to tell you,' he said.

Landry could see that he was summoning his courage. He glared at him.

'Meeting's about to start.'

'Won't take a minute,' Mick said.

A droplet of sweat ran down his temple.

Landry looked past him. More people were entering the store and finding places on the benches. Where was Joe? If fifty bucks a head couldn't make him bring in those no-goods then nothing would. Remy and Charles must have started the sweep by now. A few more minutes and Landry would have Stranger and that other guy standing right here.

Landry stared hard at Mick.

'Can't it wait?' Landry snapped.

For a moment he thought the saloon keeper would

back down. He saw him twist the filthy apron tighter in his hands.

'We're leaving,' Mick said. 'Me and Dainty. Found a wagon that will take us and we're heading west at first light.'

'What?'

'Handing over the running of the saloon to the cooks. You know how hard they work.'

'You're walking out?' Landry said. Blood rose in his face. 'Gave you the saloon to run and this is the thanks I get?'

'Thinking of Dainty,' Mick said. 'Saloon in a trail fort ain't no place for a girl to grow up.'

'Won't be a trail fort for much longer,' Landry said. 'This is going to be a boom town. You need to stay here and work for me, Mick. There ain't no future for you in California. You ain't a farmer. First hard winter you get, Dainty will starve to death. That is if the consumption or the cholera don't get her first. You'll be taking her through territories where there're outbreaks every year.'

'I've made up my mind,' Mick said.

'Everybody on the train pays a Militia Charge before the train leaves in the morning,' Landry said coldly. 'Remy and Charles will make sure of it.'

Mick let his apron fall. He looked Landry in the eye.

'You've had too much of my money already,' Mick said.

'Everyone's got to pay rent.' Landry glowered. 'Everyone needs protection.'

Mick turned to go.

'The boys will be bringing in the fella who shot Lars so you can identify him,' Landry called after him. 'Just make sure you say what you agreed with Remy. Disappoint me twice in one night, that little girl of yours will grow up an orphan.'

Mick picked up the hem of his apron again and ran it through his fingers. He avoided Landry's stare and said nothing. His solemn face was tight with worry as he edged his way back through the crowd.

Outside, Joe watched Wesley and Eve walk up to the store. Eve was wearing a man's jacket and pants and she was leading Dainty by the hand. The little girl was hidden under a plainsman's hat.

'Got that other fella with you?' Joe said.

Eve looked through him.

'You can see we ain't.'

'What are you dressed like that for?'

'Work clothes,' Eve said. 'Not that it's a concern of yours.'

They pushed past him and took their place in the queue for the door.

'They'll be finding him right about now,' Joe shouted after them. 'Just listen out for the shot. There ain't nowhere he can hide.

Inside, Wesley and Eve met up with Mick standing at the back of the room. Dainty flung her arms round her pa.

'Tell him?' Wesley said.

Mick nodded.

'How did he take it?'

Mick's putty face looked grave.

'Riled about us leavin'.' Mick's voice was hoarse. 'Talked about makin' Dainty an orphan if I don't point the finger at Stranger.'

'What's an orphan, Pa?' Dainty said.

'Someone who ain't got a ma or pa.' Mick drew her close.

'How can I be an orphan?' Dainty piped up. 'I got you.'

She gazed up at him and giggled at her pa's foolishness.

Eve gently smoothed Dainty's hair with the palm of her hand.

Wesley looked Mick in the eye.

'You do what you have to,' Wesley said. 'That's what Stranger would say. He knows what he's up against. Viperines ain't the first who have tried to get the drop on him. He won't hold nothing against you.'

Mick looked down at Dainty. He squeezed her shoulders and she smiled up at him.

'Pa, Eve says I can keep this hat after tonight.'

Some of the people who had arrived first shifted uncomfortably on their seats, waiting for the proceedings to start.

'Benches are awful hard, Landry,' someone called out. 'Ready for the get go?'

'A few minutes,' Landry said. 'Just waiting for a couple more to arrive.'

The store clock showed fifteen minutes after nine when Remy burst in. He shoved through the rows of people seated on benches till he stood beside Landry.

'Ain't found 'em,' he hissed. 'Charles is still lookin'.'

'Can't you do anything right? Just both of you get back here right now.'

Landry stood up. He held up his hand to silence the buzz of conversation.

'Two people we were waiting for ain't showed up. I got some things to say so we'll start without 'em.'

Landry reached back behind the counter and heaved out a heavy wooden board. There was an expectant murmur amongst the crowd. Remy and Charles slipped into the store and stood leaning against the door. Joe was with them.

'Things I've got to say are important,' Landry continued. 'To all of us. Whether you live here or whether you're passing through. With the troopers gone, this ain't a fort no more, this is a town. It's a town with a history: my family started a trading post here when this wasn't nothing but a wilderness of sage brush. Then the military came and turned it into a fort. In the meantime the place grew. People settled. We got a store, a livery and a saloon all because of what my family started. Now the troopers have gone and left us and this town belongs to me and my family once again.'

Landry looked round the room. The faces he saw were puzzled and grave.

'In honour of this occasion, I'm renaming this place in front of you all. I'm gonna have this sign put up at the town entrance in the morning.'

He manhandled the heavy board round to face the crowd. There, in high ox-blood capitals was the single word 'Viperine'.

12

Landry's face blazed with pride. The only sound was a rat scuffling somewhere beneath the floorboards. He held up the heavy sign and displayed it to all parts of the room. Everyone stared at the word printed in blood-coloured letters and wondered what this meant.

When enough time had passed, Landry put down the sign, slipped a stogie from his vest pocket and struck a match. There was a brief, bright splutter of phosphorous. He drew heavily on the cigar and blew a thin column of smoke over the heads of the seated crowd.

'As landlord of this town,' Landry continued, 'it's my duty to protect you. You need protection and you'll have to pay. There ain't no other way of doin' things. There's danger from the Sioux when you're outside and there's danger right here in the town itself.'

People in the crowd turned to each other. What did he mean, they'd have to pay? No one had seen the Sioux for nearly a year. And what did he mean 'danger right here'?

'Had a man in the lock-up,' Landry went on. 'He shot Lars the Norwegian.'

There were gasps in the crowd.

'I intended to bring this murderer here in front of you tonight. Viperine don't need no travelling judge when we got fair-minded folks like yourselves to act as a jury.'

'Where is this murderer?' someone shouted.

Landry smiled, took a pull on his stogie and let the ash fall on to the floor. He had won them over. His citizens. His town.

'On the loose, right here in Viperine.' Landry breathed another lungful of smoke over the crowd. 'Along with the fella who busted him out.'

'What fella?' someone from the audience cried. 'There are two of them?'

'Conspiritors,' Landry said. 'Right here.'

He waited for the crowd to take in this latest piece of information. Anxiety rose up in the room. Everyone had left the wagons unguarded – would their possessions be safe? What conspirators? Why did they kill Lars?

Landry sensed that now was the time. 'This what you pay the Militia Charge for. Protection. So you and your families can be safe right here in Viperine and on the trail outside.'

'Wait a minute,' someone called. 'How do we know one of these fellas killed Lars?'

Landry took one last draw on his stogie and ground the butt under his heel. Choking smoke wreathed around him and he coughed out his words.

'Got an eye-witness right here in this room. One of our most upstanding citizens. Chosen to bring up his little daughter here in Viperine.'

Landry beckoned Mick to step forward. Mick pushed Dainty into Eve's arms. His grey face was haggard with worry and sweat stood out on his brow.

'You know me,' he began.

'Speak up,' someone called.

Mick held the hem of his apron in his hands and searched the room for a friendly face.

'It's true I was there when Lars got shot,' he said. 'It was behind the saloon tent, right by the cooking fires.'

Mick hesitated. He wound the hem of his filthy apron tight. He caught Dainty's eye and smiled at her. People turned in their seats to follow his gaze and saw the little girl raise her hand and wave to her pa.

'I saw the man who shot him.' Mick's voice broke. 'I saw him pull the trigger.'

The crowd turned back to him. Mick was shaking. Where he twisted the apron, his knuckles were white.

'It wasn't who they said it was.'

There was a disturbance in the crowd. Landry leapt to his feet. Mick looked into his daughter's beautiful face.

'It wasn't the guy they had in the lock-up.'

'Wait!'

Someone shouted from the back of the room. A woman's voice. The crowd craned round to see. It was Eve.

'He's telling the truth. The guy in the lock-up rode in with us. He never harmed nobody.'

129

'You gonna believe her?' Landry yelled. 'She don't know nothing.'

'I busted him out of the lock-up,' Eve said. 'And I helped shut Charles Viperine in there to give him a taste of his own medicine.'

She reached down and plucked the hat off Dainty's head, shook the newspaper out of it and put it on. She turned towards the door where Charles stood beside his brother and Joe.

'Recognize me now?'

Silence stunned the room. Landry gaped at her; Mick dropped the hem of his apron; Wesley was ready to pull Eve towards him; Remy looked wildly at Landry to know what to do; Joe gawked, open mouthed; Eve shoved Dainty behind her. As Charles let out a squeal of rage, the doors to the store burst open and skittled Charles, Remy and Joe to the floor. Stranger stood there calm and still.

Mayhem. The crowd shoved, fought and shouted trying to get out of the way without knowing which direction to go or what they were trying to get away from. Joe, Remy and Charles scrambled to pick themselves up. Landry yelled something. Wesley pushed forward to stand beside Stranger but Stranger motioned him back.

Then Mick's voice broke over everything.

'I seen the man who shot Lars. I was standing right there. They wanted me to say it was this fella but it wasn't him, it was Remy Viperine.'

'Tell them, Landry,' Remy screamed. 'Tell them it wasn't me.'

Without taking his eyes off Remy, Stranger kicked the door open with his boot heel.

'Remy Viperine, I'm calling you out,' Stranger said. His voice was steel. 'For the murder of Lars the Norwegian. The murder you tried to pin on me.'

'Landry!' Remy screamed. 'Tell them!'

Stranger backed out of the store, across the porch and down the steps. When he was ten yards out into the square he stopped. He faced the door to the grocery, his hands ready over his holsters. The torchlight flickered across his bruised face. There was a weariness there as though he had played out this scene before and had hoped he would never have to again. People pressed against the window on one side of the door. The window on the other side darkened as someone moved an oil lamp back into the room to get a better view.

Remy stepped on to the porch. There was a smirk on his lips but his eyes were afraid.

'Same as always,' Stranger said. 'Count of three.'

Stranger's hands steadied over his guns. Starr double-action six-shots, the newest design money could buy, accurate over fifty yards. No need to cock the hammer to take a second shot. Not that there was ever time for a second shot.

'One,' Stranger began.

Time slowed down. Torchlight flickered over the side of the store; flames reflected off the windows and the faces of the two men. There was no sound from inside. Silence weighed on the square and the air was still. The men stared into each other's eyes, searching for the sign of an intention, the indication of a movement, anything which might give them away.

'Two.'

Remy saw nothing in Stranger's eyes. They were blank to him. How dare this outsider accuse him in front of everyone, here in his family's town? Flames of hatred burned within him. How dare this guy in his ridiculous old buckskin jacket stand there so serene? Remy was used to feeling anger but this time his rage meant that it was all he could do to keep his hand steady.

Stranger read Remy as he had read other gunfighters before. In this last moment he saw everything: Remy's refusal to back down; refusal to admit what he had done; his lying; the cheating and the bullying; the shortcuts he took; his fear of Landry and his contempt for almost everyone; most of all, his loathing for himself.

'Three.'

Stranger drew both Starrs and loosed off a round from each. Never time for a second shot. At the same time, he flung himself sideways on to the ground. Remy fired and there was a shot from the darkened store window. Remy slumped to the ground and let his pistol fall; Charles toppled through the store window, his gun in his hand.

Shouts detonated in the store. Running feet. Stranger picked himself up. Hands helped him. He pushed people away and holstered the Starrs.

'You hit?' It was Eve's voice. She was right there close to him.

He turned and smiled at her.

'Me?'

He brushed the dust off his buckskin and straightened his hat. He nodded in the direction of the porch where the bodies of Remy and Charles lay.

'Both dead,' Eve said.

'Every time I draw my gun,' Stranger said.

On the porch, the folks from the wagon train shrank back and Landry stood between the bodies of his brothers. He stared at Stranger as though he were storing everything in his memory. His face was a mask which showed neither grief nor anger; his eyes glittered as he calculated his next move. For a moment, Eve thought she saw him touch his hat to Stranger but in the bad light she couldn't be sure. Stranger made no acknowledgement.

Mick hurried down the porch steps with his arm round Dainty's shoulders.

'We're still leaving in the morning?' he said. 'This don't change nothing?'

He hurried the little girl away.

Someone spoke to Landry and a group of men set about laying sheets over the bodies and straightening the limbs ready to carry them through to the table in the back room behind the store, the place they had used before. After a while, Pa Tolson came out to supervise. Landry brushed past him and stepped back inside. Through the window, Eve saw him sit down at a table with Joe. She tensed. What were they planning?

'It's all right,' Stranger said. 'This is over.'

Stranger stood there and watched the men carry in

the two bodies as if he had to wait for the scene to end and the curtains to close.

Wesley emerged from the store and came down the steps. He stared hard at Stranger.

'You all right?'

'He's fine,' Eve said.

The temperature had fallen and the air was crisp. On the empty prairie, a wind picked up and here in the square, little cold gusts raised the dust around their feet. Above them, the cloudless night sky was a banner of stars. Their hard, silver light was beautiful and unforgiving; beyond them a swathe of galaxies were luminous and pale. Away to the west a comet slashed the sky: the diamond point burst alight, flared bright as magnesium, traced an arc and died in the velvet darkness.

'I'll speak to Landry,' Stranger said.

Wesley glanced at him. 'Want me to come with you?'

Stranger shook his head.

As Joe and Landry watched from the store window, Stranger mounted the steps. The fall had left him with a stiffness in his walk or maybe he took each step slowly to give Landry time to realize he was coming, Eve couldn't tell.

As Stranger entered, Joe went for his gun. But Landry grabbed his arm and eased it away from his holster. Stranger stood with his arms wide, palms open.

'You gonna let him—' Joe stuttered.

'Heading east at first light,' Stranger said. 'Catch a few hours' shut-eye in the livery first.'

Landry nodded.

'Just telling you so you'll know where I'll be.'

'Appreciate that,' Landry said.

'Boss, you ain't gonna—' Joe started again.

Stranger ignored Joe and spoke straight to Landry.

'Just one more thing,' he said. 'These are poor people in the wagons. They ain't got nothing except their Bibles and the clothes they're standing in. Odds are some of 'em ain't gonna make it to California alive.'

Landry shrugged.

'I want you to forget this Militia Charge.'

Stranger's words hung in the air.

'Why should I?'

'I know Joe here is itchin' to shoot me,' Stranger said. 'But these folks ain't got no one to stand for them so I guess I will. Your brothers are dead. We've had enough killing for one night.'

'Let me take him,' Joe hissed. 'There's two of us.'

'Quiet.' Landry rounded on him.

He looked at Stranger.

'My brothers had their way of doing things. Didn't do no good in the end. This is over now.'

Landry nodded to Stranger.

'You got my word.'

Stranger turned and left the store. He trod slowly down the steps and did not look back at the window from which Joe and Landry watched him. He refused Eve's offer of coffee and made his way directly to the stable.

Inside the store, Landry gestured Joe to sit down again.

'You didn't find 'em,' he said. 'I lost my brothers because of that. You owe me.'

'What Remy and Charles did wasn't my fault,' Joe protested. 'They was lookin' too and they never found that guy.'

'You stay on and work for me.' Landry looked hard at him. 'I'm gonna need a right hand now.'

'I dunno,' Joe said, careful not to catch Landry's eye. 'I want to roll up a stake, be my own boss. There's land for the taking in California. Planned to leave when the next wagon train came through.'

'Regular wage. Most guys would jump at it.'

'Worked for rich guys before,' Joe said. 'The wage they pay you is gone before you know it. You never get no stake in nothing.'

He glanced at Landry. He must be careful not to overplay his hand.

'All found,' Landry insisted. 'Place to sleep and everything.'

'What do you want me to do?'

'Collect the rents. Collect the Militia Charge when the next train comes in. Keep an eye on the saloon now Mick's quit. Things have got to change. This town has got to be run right.'

'I'll take it,' Joe said. 'Trial basis. Make a decision when the next train comes in.'

The two men shook on it.

'Any newspapers round here?' Joe said. 'I was reading one in the saloon. Never finished it.'

13

The men harnessed their horses to the wagons before daylight and made the square musical with the jingle of trace chains and the drum of hoofs on the hard ground. The air smelled of smoke and coffee and people from the wagons hurried back and forth on last-minute errands, called out morning greetings to each other and checked that their loads were fastened down.

As darkness gave way to grey pre-dawn light, Eve and Wesley led their wagon out from behind the stable. Mick waited for them with Dainty still rubbing sleep from her eyes. Eve lifted Dainty up into the back of the wagon where she had prepared a nest of blankets on the horsehair mattress. The child gratefully snuggled under the covers and slipped back into dreamland.

There was a delay but no one seemed to know what caused it. Men and women shivered by their wagons, bullwhips in their hands and blankets round their shoulders. Eve sat in the back of the wagon to watch over Dainty while Mick and Wesley waited outside.

Red flames spread across the eastern sky and gold

light glanced off the high clouds. The new daylight filled the hearts of the pioneers with hope and renewed their determination. Then word filtered down the train: one of Henry Winter's horses had a loose shoe. As his was the lead wagon, there would be an hour's delay while he did the blacksmithing. Grumbling about the hold-up, some folks rekindled their breakfast fires to brew up a last pot of coffee while others leaned back against their wagons and rolled cigarettes.

When Eve saw Stranger ride out from behind the stable, she climbed down from the back of the wagon. For a moment she thought he was going to ride right past them so she called out. He reined in his horse and rested his hands on his saddle.

'Ain't started out yet?' Stranger said.

She noted how well prepared he was. His bedding was neatly rolled behind his saddle; his Winchester was ready in its long holster; the leather laces of his saddlebags were tied and his canteen was to hand. But he looked as if sleep had not refreshed him. There were shadows under his eyes and his face was tense and pale. The old buckskin jacket which he usually kept brushed was dirty, as though he had dropped it in the mud and not noticed.

He smiled down at Eve. His calm, grey eyes registered her concern for him.

'Got the child with you?'

Eve's attention was immediately distracted.

'She's sleeping,' Eve said. She smiled at the thought of Dainty in the back of their wagon.

Landry and Joe surveyed the wagons from the

vantage point of the store porch under the new Viperine sign. Both men had their Colts strapped to their hips. When people from the wagons caught their eye, they looked away. Eventually Landry became bored and headed back inside. Joe pulled up a wooden chair and continued to stare at the train. Eve noticed him watching her.

'Want me to wait till you pull out?' Stranger said.

'It's all right,' Eve said. She smiled at him. 'If you're heading out, always start at dawn.'

Wesley and Mick noticed them and came over.

'Fine morning.' Stranger touched the brim of his hat.

He clicked his tongue and the horse moved forward. Wesley started to say something but Stranger was gone. They watched him ride past the saloon tent, through the gates of the stockade and head out on to the prairie. His horse's pace was strong and steady and Stranger held himself upright in the saddle. The people from the wagons were making the most of the delay by chatting as they waited for coffee to boil. As Stranger spoke to no one, few of them noticed him leave.

Joe did. He swung his feet up on the porch rail and leaned back in his chair. He studied Stranger's progress as he crossed the square and then stood up to watch him ride out into the prairie as if he wanted to be sure.

'Didn't say goodbye,' Eve said quietly.

'Told me once,' Wesley said, 'start early in the morning and never say goodbye.'

All three of them stared after him.

'Never saw anyone draw so fast,' Wesley said. 'Both guns at the same time. Didn't even have a clear view of the guy in the window and he still got the drop on him. Where does someone learn to shoot like that?'

'Two of them,' Mick added. 'And he just walked away. Never seen anything like it.'

'Didn't want money,' Wesley reflected. 'Didn't stick around long enough for anyone to thank him.'

'They wouldn't have let him leave,' Eve said. 'Not after they tried to pin Lars' murder on him. He had to face 'em down.'

'Could have just saddled up and hightailed it,' Mick reflected. 'Once you'd busted him out. Wasn't slowed down by a wagon and he didn't have to think of no one else. That's what I would have done.'

'That wasn't a choice for him,' Wesley said. 'Don't reckon he's run out on nothing his whole life.'

'Still can't get over how he drilled two of 'em and walked away without a scratch,' Mick said.

Without warning, Eve turned and strode off towards the stable. Mick and Wesley stared after her.

'Where's she going?' Wesley said.

'Tell you one thing while she ain't around.' Mick lowered his voice and leaned towards Wesley. 'That guy with the newspaper on the porch has been staring over this way for quite a while.'

'Joe?'

'Reckon he's gonna try something?' Mick said.

'Ain't got Remy and Charles to back him up now,' Wesley said.

He looked back towards the store. Joe had propped

his boots on the rail again. He held Wesley's stare.

'Still reckons Eve should rightfully be with him,' Mick said.

'Reckon if he tried to take her back, she'd shoot him right off. Don't know why she ain't done that already.'

'Stands up for herself,' Mick said. 'I can see that.'

'She ain't afraid of no one,' Wesley said. 'Not now.'

'She always been like that?'

'When I met her she'd took another name,' Wesley said. 'I didn't know it but she was running out on Joe. I liked her straight off: she looked me in the eye and spoke straight. Only thing was she tried to hide that scar Joe gave her. Used to pull her hair down over her face. Used to tie her cotton bonnet real tight.'

Wesley smiled.

'She was scared I wouldn't take her with me because of a mark on her face.' He laughed at the thought. 'When we bust the axle, she wouldn't come into the fort because she didn't want nobody to see her.'

'Ain't like that now,' Mick said. 'Ain't afraid of nothing.'

'That's right,' Wesley said. 'That's how Eve's been since she met Stranger. Guess we've all been stronger since we met him. He told me a story once about how the trail judges you. There ain't no law out here, no rules for folks to weasel round like there are back East. There's only right and wrong under a wide open sky. You do what you do and the trail shows you who you are. He called that "trail judgement". Reckon he told her that story.'

'If we were back East,' Mick said, 'Some court would

send her back to Joe even after what he done.'

Mick and Wesley broke off talking when they saw Eve approach.

'Look at this.'

She held out a fistful of straw she had gathered in the stable.

'There's blood on it.'

Wesley took the straw from her and picked it apart.

'It's from the place Stranger was sleeping.'

It took a second for them to realize.

'He got shot?' Wesley said.

'He walked away,' Mick said. 'Why didn't he say nothing?'

They looked at each other.

'Reckon we should go after him?' Mick went on.

They all knew the answer.

'How come you figured that out?' Wesley said.

'Mark on his jacket,' Eve said. 'Saw it this morning but I only just realized.'

'Reckon he'll be all right?' Wesley said. 'Could have a slug in him.'

'Never said goodbye,' Mick said. 'To any of us.'

In the east, the sun ignited the sky and lit the feather traces of cloud which arched over the prairie. They thought of Stranger alone out there amongst the sage-brush, riding hundreds of miles home to make peace with a brother who might not want to know him and a woman who probably wished she never had. And doing it because he knew it was right.

'Wouldn't want us to go after him,' Eve said. 'I'm sure of that.'

Henry Winter paced the length of the train. He took big strides and waved to the wagons as he passed, a confident beam on his thin, weather-beaten face. He relished his role as leader of the wagon train and with everyone ready to move out, his heart sang.

'Won't be long now.'

He called cheerful greetings and apologies for the delay to each wagon. When he came to Wesley and Mick he stopped.

'Where's that little girl?' he said. 'You ain't left her behind?'

Mick laughed.

'Wouldn't do that.'

Eve went round to check on Dainty and climbed in to the wagon to sit with her.

'Flat country and the ground's firm. Should make ten miles by sundown, even with this delay,' Winter said. ''Course it's the ox carts slow us down. Those beauties are strong enough to pull anything but if you drive 'em on too fast, their hearts give out. Seen that happen. A team can be under the yoke one minute and on their knees the next. Ain't no warning.'

As Henry Winter turned to go, someone called out to him from the direction of the store. His smile vanished.

'Hey, Winter.'

Joe hurried towards them waving a rolled newspaper.

'Read the news?'

'Ain't had time.'

Henry Winter's dislike for Joe was evident. He had done that terrible thing to his own wife, showed not the slightest remorse and taken advantage of the good people on the train. Winter expected Joe to quote some article about an Indian attack on a wagon train or some outbreak of disease at a trail fort, anything to try to dampen his enthusiasm for the journey. But it was nothing like that.

'You threw me off the train for not telling you my story,' Joe said. 'Reckon you might have to do that to somebody else.'

Winter glared at him.

'Before there is forgiveness there has to be repentance. We were ready to forgive but you—'

Joe cut him short.

'Look at this.'

He unfolded the newspaper and flattened out the front page. The headline read 'Bennet Fisher Escapes, Reward $1,000'.

'Why are you showing me this?' Winter snapped.

Joe ignored him and started to read.

'A man, identified as Bennet Fisher robbed the Emigrant Savings Bank in East Street, New York yesterday. Fisher was identified by his mother, Mrs Alice Fisher who happened to be in the branch at the time. In trying to get away, Fisher shot and killed the bounty hunter, Jake Turner, who was on Fisher's trail and had followed him into the bank.

'Fisher's mother said, "The other man grabbed me by the throat and pointed his revolver at my head. He shouted to Bennet that I would get it if he did not give himself up. That's when Bennet shot him."

'In the confusion after the shooting, a number of other bank customers heard Mrs Fisher shout "Run

Bennet, run." This is how Fisher was identified.

'Later when questioned, Mrs Fisher said that her son had been driven to shoot by the cowardly act of the bounty hunter. She said she knew Fisher would be sorry things had ended this way as he had never intended to kill anyone. She asked how it could be a crime for a son to protect his own mother. Mrs Fisher also denied that she had been a part of the plan to rob the bank.'

'What are you reading me this for?' Winter said. 'This is stale news and it don't concern me.'

'Wait,' Joe snapped. 'You'll see how it concerns you.'

He continued reading. 'The Emigrant Savings Bank has suffered a spate of robberies in recent weeks. On hearing of these events, the bank president, Arnold Lipman announced that he would offer a reward of $1,000 for the killing or capture of Bennet Fisher and that he sent condolences on behalf of the bank to the family of Mr Turner.'

Joe looked up at Winter. A satisfied sneer played on his lips as he turned over the page. Winter gasped in disbelief and snatched the paper out of Joe's hands. An etching of Wesley's face stared up at him. Winter turned to Wesley with questions on his lips. It was too late. Joe fired three times. Point blank range. Each round caught Wesley in the chest. Blood spattered over Henry Winter and Mick. Wesley's body convulsed after each shot and slid down the side of the wagon.

'I'm rolling up a stake,' Joe said. 'Putting this guy in my wagon and heading back to Independence. From there I can send word back to the bank in New York.'

There were shouts. Landry appeared on the porch

outside the store. People from the train called out to see if Winter was all right. Winter and Mick stared in horror at the splashes of blood on each other's faces and clothes.

Joe looked up at Henry Winter again almost as if he was seeking approval.

'Reward's right there in black and white. Anyone can see,' Joe said. 'Ain't done nothing illegal.'

The wagon rocked as Eve leapt over the tailboard. Her Patterson five-shot was trained on Joe.

'Ain't no law out here,' she said. 'Just right and wrong.'

She fired before Joe could go for his gun. Five times, until the chamber was empty.

Then Landry was there, together with a crowd from the wagons. Pa Tolson came running out of the store. Eve shoved the empty Patterson back in her belt as Dainty clambered over the tailboard of the wagon, tears streaming down her face. The little girl dived at Mick, threw her arms around his waist and buried her head in him. The blood-soaked newspaper lay at their feet.

No one spoke for a while. There were no questions to ask. Everyone could see what had happened. The men in the crowd removed their hats and they all stood still. Some bowed their heads, others stared at Eve. Her face was calm and grave. The moments they stood there seemed unending. The only sounds were Dainty's sobs and the only movement was the pages of the newspaper which curled in the breeze.

Mick cleared his throat. 'Why didn't he go for his gun?'

'Wasn't quick enough,' Landry said. 'Joe shot him before he could draw.'

'No,' Mick said. 'It wasn't that.'

They all looked down at Wesley's body where he had fallen against the wagon. His Colt was still in its holster. His right hand was reaching into his jacket. Eve cried out softly and knelt beside him. She gently lifted the front of his coat. Wesley's hand held a blood-soaked envelope, half removed from his inside pocket. On the front of the envelope in careful copperplate, Wesley had written her name.

14

Henry-Winter eventually led the wagons out at midday. As the mules and oxen took the strain and the wheels creaked on their axles, everyone came out to see them off. The Chinese cooks lined up outside the saloon tent and the Tolsons stood on the porch in front of the store. During the morning, the guys with ladders returned and took down the Viperine sign over the door.

'Gonna be called Tolson's like it always was,' Pa Tolson called as Mick led the horses past. 'When you said you were leaving, Landry made me an offer. That was one of my terms.'

From the driver's seat with Eve's hat planted on her head, Dainty blew kisses to Ma Tolson. Eve sat one side of Dainty and on the other her arm circled the jar of boiled sugars, the contents of which were almost untouched.

Eve was slumped against the sideboard of the wagon as if some yoke was pressing down on her shoulders which made the effort of sitting upright too much. Her face was washed out, her hair scraped back and her eyes stared into some unseen distance. There was redness along her eyelids but she had fought back tears. The Patterson was still stuffed in her belt and in her hand, she clutched the bloodstained envelope.

Ma Tolson called out to her, but Eve did not hear. Mick looked across at her. Daisy moved close and rested her cheek against Eve's shoulder.

'She'll be all right,' Mick called. 'Me and Dainty will make sure of it.'

Pa Tolson climbed down off the porch to walk beside Mick.

'Tell her I'll see to all the arrangements,' he said. 'It'll be done decent.'

Mick nodded.

'She'll make a new start in California. We all will.'

Pa Tolson wasn't able to contain himself any longer.

'Landry's promised me the store,' he burst out. 'Freehold land, building. Won't have no rent to pay.'

'What brought this on?' Mick said.

'Reckons we can build a town here, with more trains coming through every year. I reckon he's right. He wants me and Ma to stay and he wants settlers here. Ain't no need for everyone to head out to California. Says we won't attract them if the place is a rough house. We got to run it right. Wants me to help him.'

Mick listened carefully.

'Remy had a habit of stirring things up when they ought to be left alone. With him gone, I reckon you've got a chance.'

'What about you?' Tolson said.

'I'm through with the saloon business,' Mick said. 'While there's still land claims going, I'll build a place and start a farm. Got to have somewhere Dainty can grow up and be proud of.'

Tolson could see a new confidence in Mick as he marched along beside the horses. Where Mick's surly face had always looked anxious and his temper was short, now there was calm determination in the way he spoke of his future plans. Getting away from the bullying Viperines, out of the steam and grease of the kitchen and striding towards his own destiny suited him.

Then there was Dainty. She leaned against Eve to comfort her until some detail caught her attention then she sat bolt upright and stared. Everything interested her. It could be something in the wagons up ahead: the angle of a turning wheel, the way sunlight glanced off a canvas bonnet or the gait of the men and women walking alongside their horses. Too young to remember the journey which had brought her to Fort Dove, everything was fresh and new to her and held depths of mystery waiting to be uncovered.

Pa Tolson waved goodbye to them at the stockade. He stood and watched the wagons head out into the sage until they shrank to the size of toys. He was used to wagon trains coming and going, to greetings and goodbyes but he would miss Mick and Ma would miss Dainty. But the place was going to change and that gave him hope. Mick was right: without Remy and Charles, Landry would have to rely on good will to run the town. To make sure of that, he would have to treat people right. They would all have the chance to prosper.

Eve barely spoke. She sat slumped against the side of the wagon all day and in the evening unrolled the horsehair mattress in the back, wrapped herself in blankets and lay down. Despite Mick's encouragement and Dainty's pleas, she hardly ate. When she looked at Dainty, her usual warmth was replaced by distance as if she was seeing her from far away. She knew Dainty's affection was there because she could see her smiling face but with her heart frozen by grief she felt nothing.

Dainty was patient. She held Eve's hand and waited.

As the days rolled on and the Rockies came into view, Eve climbed down from the wagon and walked beside Mick. Often Dainty joined her and soon Eve found the little girl's cheerful chatter as infectious as she always had. The great weight began to lift off her. She began to laugh again as Dainty cartwheeled alongside them, sang songs with her, joined her in spotting jackrabbits and naming the birds which soared overhead. Mick watched as Dainty brought Eve back to herself.

Throughout all this time, Eve either held the envelope in her hand or had it close in the pocket of her jacket. Occasionally Mick noticed her rereading it or running the tip of her finger over the bloodstains on the envelope which were now lusterless and drab. He never asked and she never confided in him.

One afternoon, Eve and Mick walked side by side with the mountains rearing ahead of them and the prairie sage brushing their boots. The bright sun made the day glorious. Daisy had exhausted herself cartwheeling and was asleep in the wagon. Eve started to talk about Wesley.

'Get the chance to say much to him?'

'Never got to know him well,' Mick said. 'Saw he had a fondness for you.'

'Yes, he did,' Eve said. 'Did he tell you how we met?'

She told the story of how she had answered Wesley's advertisement in the *New York News* and met him in the Grapevine Coffee House. She said she had tried to hide the scar on her cheek but that Wesley saw it right away and that after they had spoken only a few words, he asked her to go out West with him. Words tumbled out of her as if by talking she could live the scene again.

'Each of us invented new names,' Eve said. 'We became the people we chose to be. By becoming someone else we could truly be ourselves.'

She looked over at Mick to see if he understood.

'Reckon Stranger knew,' she went on. 'If he didn't know, he understood. He could see the reasons for the way things are. Recognized what you should do but he never blamed you if you didn't find a way to do it.'

A heat haze danced over the prairie and bent the air so the mountains seemed at once near and far away. Eve pulled down her hat against the glare of the sun. The wagon creaked and jolted and the horses' iron shod footfalls pounded the hard ground. Dainty slept through it all.

'With Stranger there, I knew what I had to do,' Mick reflected. 'That night in the store in front of Dainty, I couldn't tell those lies.'

'You did right,' Eve said.

Mick smiled ruefully.

'Surprised myself,' he said. 'Ain't never been a courageous man.'

'One day I'll tell Dainty,' Eve said. 'I'll make sure she knows her father was brave and she can be proud.'

Dainty poked her head round the bonnet of the wagon. Her eyes sparkled with delight at the afternoon.

'Want to sing some songs?' Dainty said.

'I'll sing with you,' Eve said. 'We both will. What's your favourite?

That evening, with the wagons in a circle and the cooking fires dying down, Dainty played a wild game of chase with the children from the other wagons. Eve sat with Mick and gazed up at the stars.

'When we get to California,' Eve said, 'we can build two cabins side by side. One for you and Dainty and a smaller one for me.'

Mick grinned. Lately, they'd been having this conversation every night.

'We'll pick a parcel of land where a valley opens out below us and there's enough space for the cabins, a yard and a corral for the horses.'

'Cattle,' Mick said. 'We'll keep the cattle in the valley where the grazing is rich. Beefs mainly but we'll keep a milk cow in the pasture behind the house for our milk and butter. And away to one side we'll have a pen for the hogs. Far enough away so we can't smell 'em from the house.'

Mick closed his eyes so he could see the place better.

'Behind the house we'll have the orchard, lemon trees, apricots, oranges and apples.'

'Chickens in the yard,' Eve said. 'That's going to be Dainty's first job, feeding the chickens. After that I'll teach her to milk the cow.'

'And bees,' Mick said. 'We'll have a hive of bees in a wild flower meadow somewhere so we can just reach in and take the honeycomb right out.'

They laughed at themselves just as they did every time they told this story.

Every day as the wheels of their wagon rolled closer to the promised land, Eve believed more and more strongly that their dream would become real but Mick's confidence began to falter. They began to discuss practical considerations and the more they talked, the more skeptical Mick became. His old anxiety returned and once again he became the putty-faced saloon cook struggling under the weight of expectations from his boss and the demands of his customers.

'It'll be hard work,' Mick said. 'Just building cabins. First off we'll have to source the timber.'

'If we find the right piece of land, the timber will be right there waiting for us,' Eve countered.

'Might not find the land,' Mick said. 'I heard most of the Sierra's been torn up by gold prospectors. Ain't hardly a square inch left.'

'We'll find it. California's big enough for us and the prospectors,' Eve said. 'And I tell you one thing. If we find a gold seam running under our land, we just leave it there and don't tell no one. We ain't doing this to be greenback millionaires, we're making the best life we can for you, me and Dainty.'

'What about tools?' Mick went on. 'How are we going

to afford all the tools? Even if we get 'em, how are we gonna cut down trees with just the two of us?'

'We'll go down to Sacramento and buy all the saws and everything we need,' Eve insisted. 'We'll hire a couple of guys to fell the timber for us and while they're doing it we'll start planting the orchard. We'll build the corral and I'll find a breed mare. You can start to build up a herd. Till the cabins are built, we'll live out of the wagon just like we do now.'

'More like we'll have to get jobs in some mining camp kitchen so we can buy what we need to get started,' Mick said. 'Never wanted to do that again. Hiring guys, how are we going to pay for that?'

Mick stared into the dying fire. The embers glowed in a circle of ash.

'Maybe all we've been doing is discussing a pipe dream,' he said. 'Maybe it ain't never going to happen.'

'Why not?' Eve said.

'Things ain't exactly worked out so far,' Mick said. 'My wife died and I spent five years working for the Viperines. Should have headed west but I never did. And look what's happened to you.'

'Me?' Eve said. 'I'm heading to California just like I always intended.'

'Where are we going to get that stake?' Mick said. 'Even if we do find the land?'

'We got the stake,' Eve said quietly.

She slipped her hand inside her jacket and brought out Wesley's envelope. The edge was split open and the paper was weakened with constant handling.

'I ain't going to read it all,' Eve said.

155

A catch in her voice made Mick look up.

'Dear Eve,' she began. 'If you are reading this I guess that means I ain't around any more. I thought maybe this would happen as things have a way of catching up with you. When that wagon train rolled in and Joe was on it, I had the feeling that he was coming after you and wasn't about to let me stand in his way.

'That day we met at the Grapevine I knew you weren't who you said. You answered my questions too quick and you were just too keen to get on the trail. All you told me about your family was that you were born on a farm; you never asked where I was from or anything about me. That made me sure right from the get go. Anyhow, that didn't matter to me as I guess you have found out by now. All I wanted was someone I could trust and someone to provide cover for me in case the law came looking. It was only later on, after I got to know you. . . .' Eve put the letter down in her lap. 'I ain't going to read the next part.'

Her voice was suddenly hoarse and she avoided catching Mick's eye. She scanned the page and cleared her throat before reading on.

'I hope you've still got the wagon and all my possessions because I want you to look in my trunk. Now you've taken to wearing men's clothes there's a spare pair of boots in there which would fit you if you stuffed them out, so keep them. The shirt and jacket will be too big so you can pass them on to someone.

'Most important, there's a tin box in there with a thousand dollars in it. I ain't saying how I came by it so you won't have any crazy thoughts about returning it as

156

I know what a strong conscience you have. I want you to have the money to start your new life. As I said, the way I came by it wasn't honest but the way I'm giving it to you is. Maybe the two cancel each other out – I hope so.'

Eve read on in silence. When she looked up her eyes were wet.

'Can't read the next part,' she said.

Across the circle of wagons, Dainty, still wearing Eve's hat stuffed with newspaper, let out a joyous shriek as she raced after the other children. Mick stoked the embers of the dying fire and sat back to watch the flames catch.

'Anyhow,' Eve read. 'Take care, my dear Eve. I know what your real name is but I ain't going to use it. Best stick to the names we gave ourselves. After all, what counts is not who you were but who you want to be. I wish I could be with you. Yours with affection, Wesley.'

Eve put down the letter, tipped the envelope until a small key fell into her hand. She stared up at the jewelled sky.

Inside the wagon, Eve unearthed Wesley's trunk from under their pile of belongings.

'Can't believe you never looked in it,' Mick said.

'Had to wait till the time was right.'

Eve lifted out blankets, a linen sheet and a shirt and jacket she could remember Wesley wearing. Underneath them were his spare boots and the tin box. Eve fitted the key into the lock. Inside, there was a black tin tray with compartments for different coins. She heard Mick draw in his breath sharply. Eve's hand shook and Mick leaned over her shoulder to see. Her heart raced as she lifted the tray to uncover the place where the bills were kept. The box was empty.

Mick sat back, laughed good naturedly.

'Too much to hope for, I reckon.'

He smiled at Eve. If he was disappointed, he didn't show it.

'Never figured him as a practical joker.'

'Guess he spent it on something,' Eve said.

Puzzled, she turned her attention to the clothes and held up the shirt.

'This fit you?'

'If you don't mind me having it,' Mick said.

'Take the jacket too,' Eve said. 'Boots are nice but they're too big for me.'

Eve pulled off one of the boots she was wearing and shoved her foot in Wesley's boot and shuffled a few steps along the floor of the wagon.

'Even if I packed 'em real tight I couldn't walk in these.' Eve laughed. 'He knew I had small feet. Look at this.'

She kicked off her second boot and plunged her foot in the other half of Wesley's pair. She immediately pulled out her foot and up-ended the boot. A tight roll of bills fell out on the wagon floor.

'Used to covering his tracks,' Mick said. 'Reckon he figured you'd try those on when there wasn't no one around.'

Eve picked up the bills.

'Whatever else he did, he left us seed corn for the future.'

'You,' Mick said. 'He left it for you.'

Eve looked down at the discarded boots.

'Yes, he did.'

There was a clatter outside. Crimson-faced, breathless and with the hat making her ears stick out, Dainty scrambled up over the tailboard.

'Can I stay out a while longer, Pa?'

'You still wearing that hat?' Mick laughed.

'Eve gave it to me,' Dainty said indignantly. 'Besides that, it's the best hat in the world and it's the only one I want to wear.'

'Well in that case,' Mick said. 'You can stay out a while longer.'

With Dainty's and the other children's voices echoing between the wagons, Eve folded Wesley's clothes and packed them away again.

'Dainty's the real future,' Eve said. 'Wesley would have agreed with that. Our two cabins would be mighty quiet if there wasn't Dainty to run between them.'

Eve and Mick filed their land claim as the first snows fell. All winter they huddled under blankets in the wagon and planned the farm. Mick and Dainty walked through the woods and marked the trees to be felled for the cabins; Eve worked out how they would divert the stream to bring spring water close to the houses and they all started to clear scrub away from a south-facing rise where they would plant the orchard. Mick cut wooden stakes and they drove them into the hard ground to show where the cabins would stand.

On bright days when the air was crisp and Mick took

Dainty off to explore, Eve often stood in the middle of the rectangle of snowy grass where they would build her cabin in the spring. She imagined where the stove would be and in her mind saw the shelves which held the cooking pans and crocks of rice and flour. Her bed would be along one wall and there would be a table and chairs beneath a window, which overlooked the valley. The view would be over the whole spread. In years to come, Eve would stand there and see Mick tend his herd on the lower slopes and watch Dainty gallop her pony through the sea of rye grass.

In pride of place beside the window, Eve intended to hang the triptych: the letter, the newspaper cutting and the photograph. And one day when Dainty asked what made her turn aside and pretend to examine the studio aspidistra instead of looking straight at the camera, she would tell her.